GOSCINNY AND UDERZO

PRESENT

An Asterix Adventure

ASTERIX
AND THE
SECRET WEAPON

Written and Illustrated by ALBERT UDERZO

Translated by ANTHEA BELL *and* DEREK HOCKRIDGE

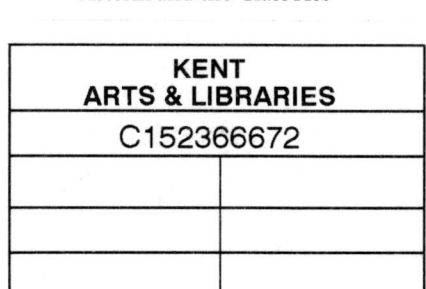

Asterix titles available now

1 Asterix the Gaul
2 Asterix and the Golden Sickle
3 Asterix and the Goths
4 Asterix the Gladiator
5 Asterix and the Banquet
6 Asterix and Cleopatra
7 Asterix and the Big Fight
8 Asterix in Britain
9 Asterix and the Normans
10 Asterix the Legionary
11 Asterix and the Chieftain's Shield
12 Asterix at the Olympic Games
13 Asterix and the Cauldron
14 Asterix in Spain
15 Asterix and the Roman Agent
16 Asterix in Switzerland
17 The Mansions of the Gods
18 Asterix and the Laurel Wreath
19 Asterix and the Soothsayer
20 Asterix in Corsica
21 Asterix and Caesar's Gift
22 Asterix and the Great Crossing
23 Obelix and Co.
24 Asterix in Belgium
25 Asterix and the Great Divide
26 Asterix and the Black Gold
27 Asterix and Son
28 Asterix and the Magic Carpet
29 Asterix and the Secret Weapon
30 Asterix and Obelix All at Sea
31 Asterix and the Actress

Asterix and the Class Act

Coming soon

Asterix versus Caesar
The Twelve Tasks of Asterix
Asterix Conquers America
Operation Getafix

Original title: *La Rose et le Glaive*

Reprinted in November 2004

Exclusive Licensee: Orion Publishing Group Ltd
Translators: Anthea Bell and Derek Hockridge
Typography: Bryony Newhouse

This edition first published in 2002 by Orion Books Ltd
Orion House, 5 Upper St Martin's Lane, London WC2H 9EA

Printed in Italy

http://gb.asterix.com
www.orionbooks.co.uk

A CIP catalogue record for this book is available from the British Library

ISBN 0 75284 716 3 (cased)
ISBN 0 75284 777 5 (paperback)

Distributed in the United States of America by Sterling Publishing Co., Inc.
387 Park Avenue South, New York, NY 10016-8810

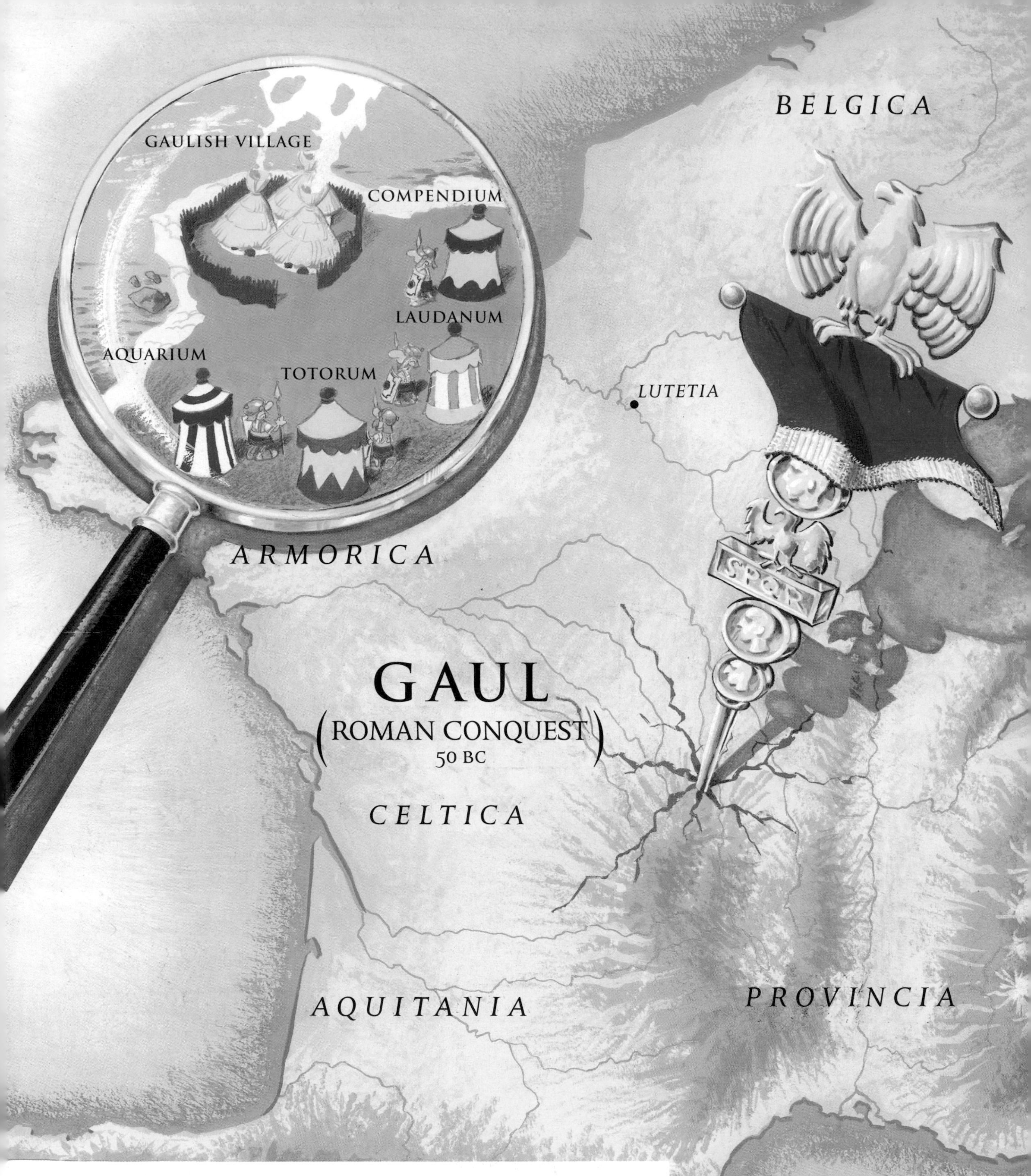
GAULISH VILLAGE
COMPENDIUM
LAUDANUM
AQUARIUM
TOTORUM
BELGICA
LUTETIA
ARMORICA
SPQR
GAUL
(ROMAN CONQUEST)
50 BC
CELTICA
AQUITANIA
PROVINCIA

THE YEAR IS 50 BC. GAUL IS ENTIRELY OCCUPIED BY THE ROMANS. WELL, NOT ENTIRELY . . . ONE SMALL VILLAGE OF THE INDOMITABLE GAULS STILL HOLDS OUT AGAINST THE INVADERS. AND LIFE IS NOT EASY FOR THE ROMAN LEGIONARIES WHO GARRISON THE FORTIFIED CAMPS OF TOTORUM, AQUARIUM, LAUDANUM AND COMPENDIUM . . .

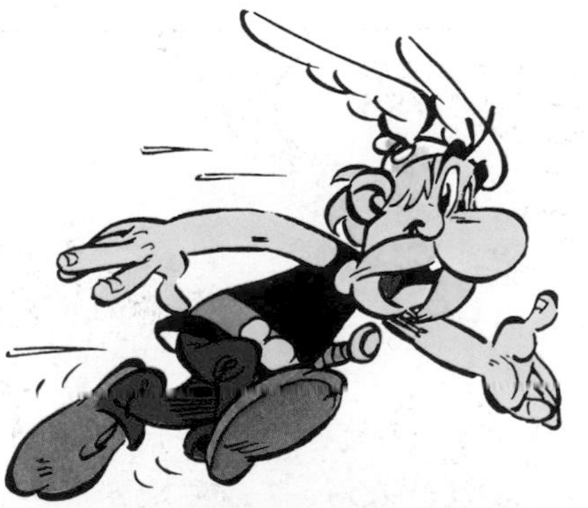

ASTERIX, THE HERO OF THESE ADVENTURES. A SHREWD, CUNNING LITTLE WARRIOR, ALL PERILOUS MISSIONS ARE IMMEDIATELY ENTRUSTED TO HIM. ASTERIX GETS HIS SUPERHUMAN STRENGTH FROM THE MAGIC POTION BREWED BY THE DRUID GETAFIX . . .

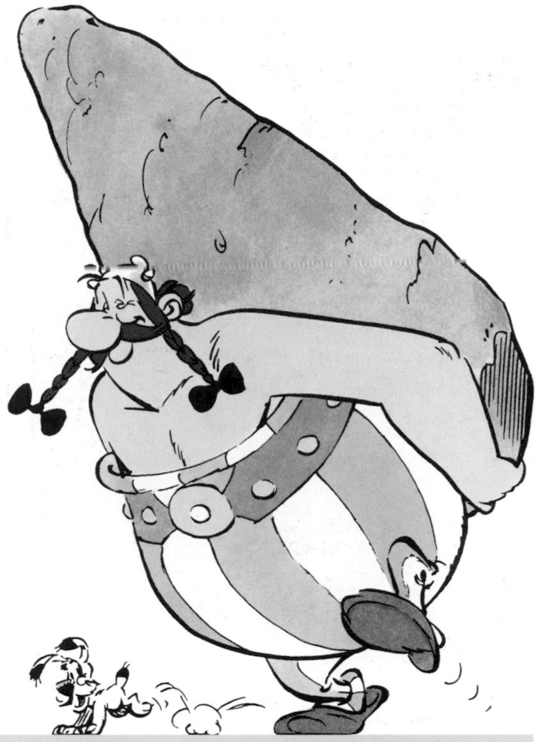

OBELIX, ASTERIX'S INSEPARABLE FRIEND. A MENHIR DELIVERY-MAN BY TRADE, ADDICTED TO WILD BOAR. OBELIX IS ALWAYS READY TO DROP EVERYTHING AND GO OFF ON A NEW ADVENTURE WITH ASTERIX – SO LONG AS THERE'S WILD BOAR TO EAT, AND PLENTY OF FIGHTING. HIS CONSTANT COMPANION IS DOGMATIX, THE ONLY KNOWN CANINE ECOLOGIST, WHO HOWLS WITH DESPAIR WHEN A TREE IS CUT DOWN.

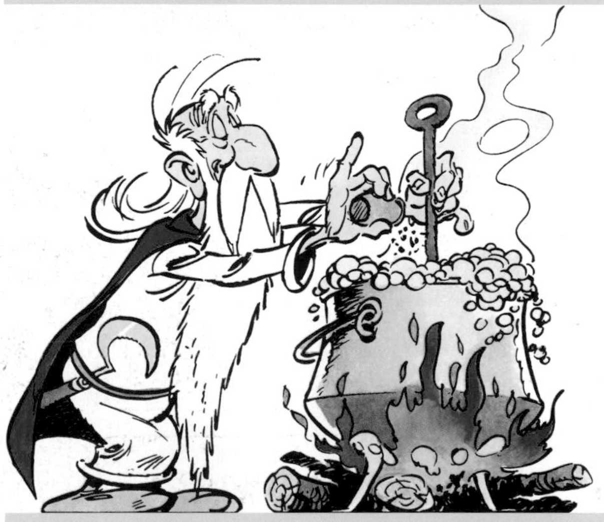

GETAFIX, THE VENERABLE VILLAGE DRUID, GATHERS MISTLETOE AND BREWS MAGIC POTIONS. HIS SPECIALITY IS THE POTION WHICH GIVES THE DRINKER SUPERHUMAN STRENGTH. BUT GETAFIX ALSO HAS OTHER RECIPES UP HIS SLEEVE . . .

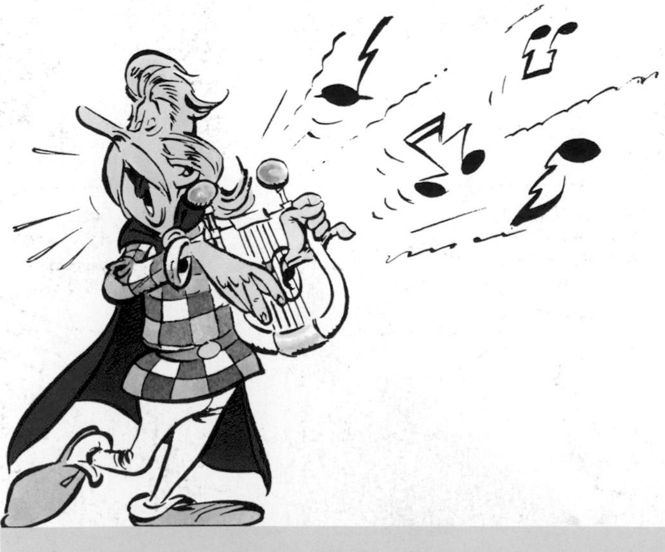

CACOFONIX, THE BARD. OPINION IS DIVIDED AS TO HIS MUSICAL GIFTS. CACOFONIX THINKS HE'S A GENIUS. EVERYONE ELSE THINKS HE'S UNSPEAKABLE. BUT SO LONG AS HE DOESN'T SPEAK, LET ALONE SING, EVERYBODY LIKES HIM . . .

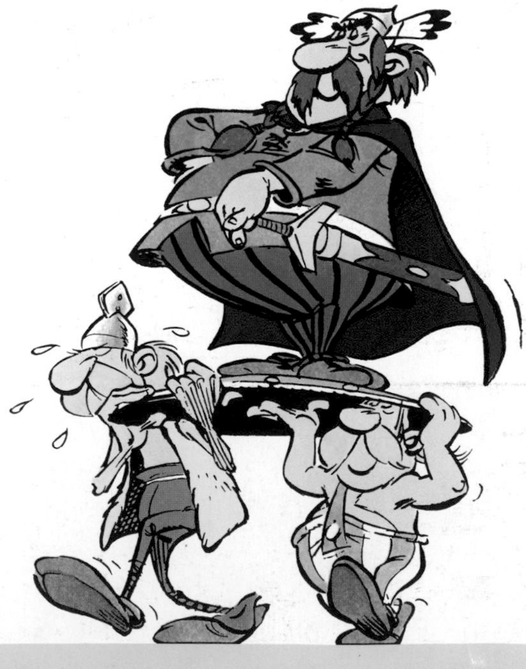

FINALLY, VITALSTATISTIX, THE CHIEF OF THE TRIBE. MAJESTIC, BRAVE AND HOT-TEMPERED, THE OLD WARRIOR IS RESPECTED BY HIS MEN AND FEARED BY HIS ENEMIES. VITALSTATISTIX HIMSELF HAS ONLY ONE FEAR, HE IS AFRAID THE SKY MAY FALL ON HIS HEAD TOMORROW. BUT AS HE ALWAYS SAYS, TOMORROW NEVER COMES.

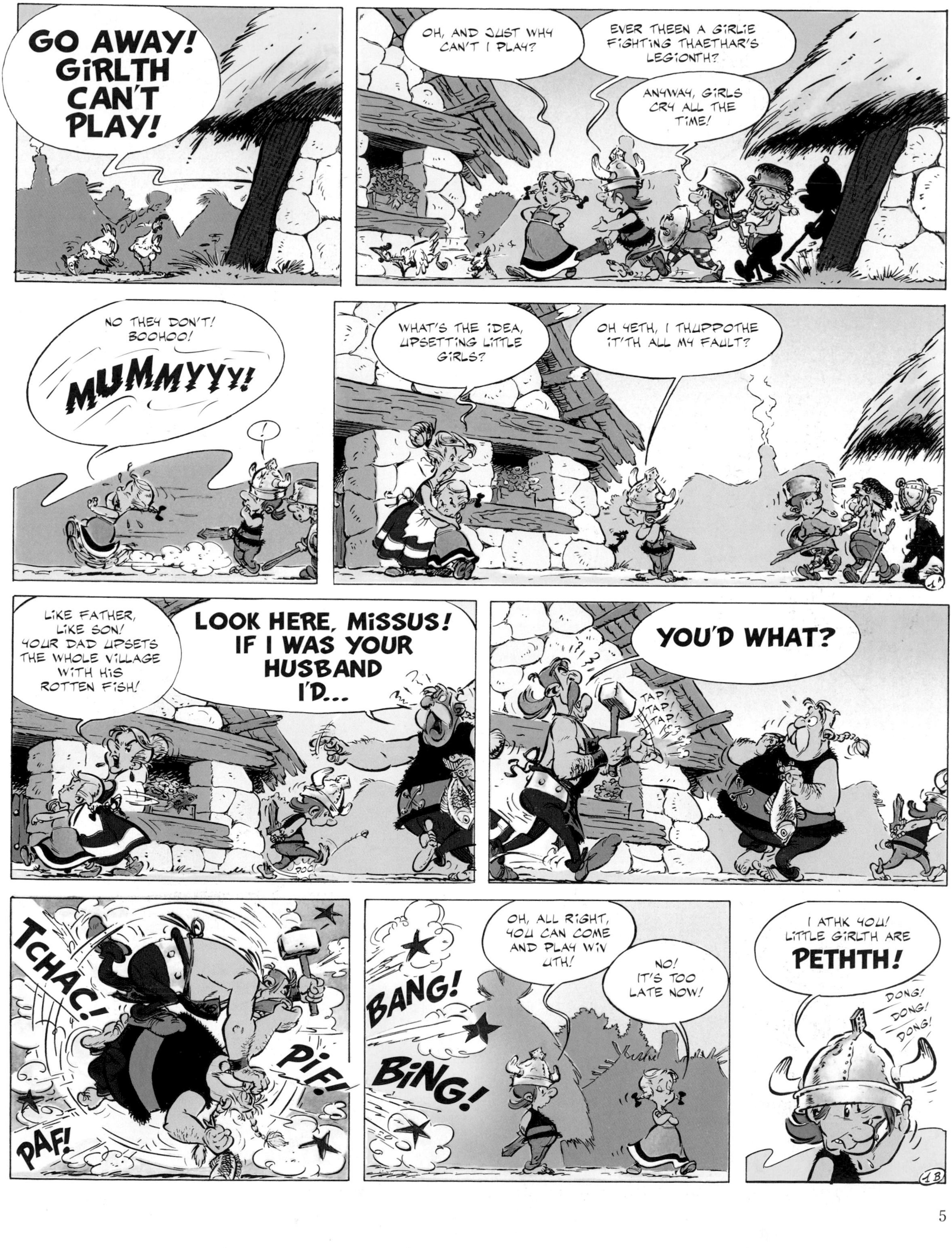
GO AWAY! GiRLTH CAN'T PLAY!
CLUCK?
OH, AND JUST WHY CAN'T I PLAY?
EVER THEEN A GiRLiE FiGHTiNG THAETHAR'S LEGiONTH?
ANYWAY, GiRLS CRY ALL THE TiME!
NO THEY DON'T! BOOHOO!
MUMMYYY!
!
WHAT'S THE iDEA, UPSETTiNG LiTTLE GiRLS?
OH YETH, I THUPPOTHE iT'TH ALL MY FAULT?
LiKE FATHER, LiKE SON! YOUR DAD UPSETS THE WHOLE ViLLAGE WiTH HiS ROTTEN FiSH!
LOOK HERE, MiSSUS! iF I WAS YOUR HUSBAND I'D...
YOU'D WHAT?
TAP! TAP! TAP!
TCHAC!
PiF!
PAF!
OH, ALL RiGHT, YOU CAN COME AND PLAY WiV UTH!
NO! iT'S TOO LATE NOW!
BANG!
BiNG!
I ATHK YOU! LiTTLE GiRLTH ARE PETHTH!
DONG! DONG! DONG!

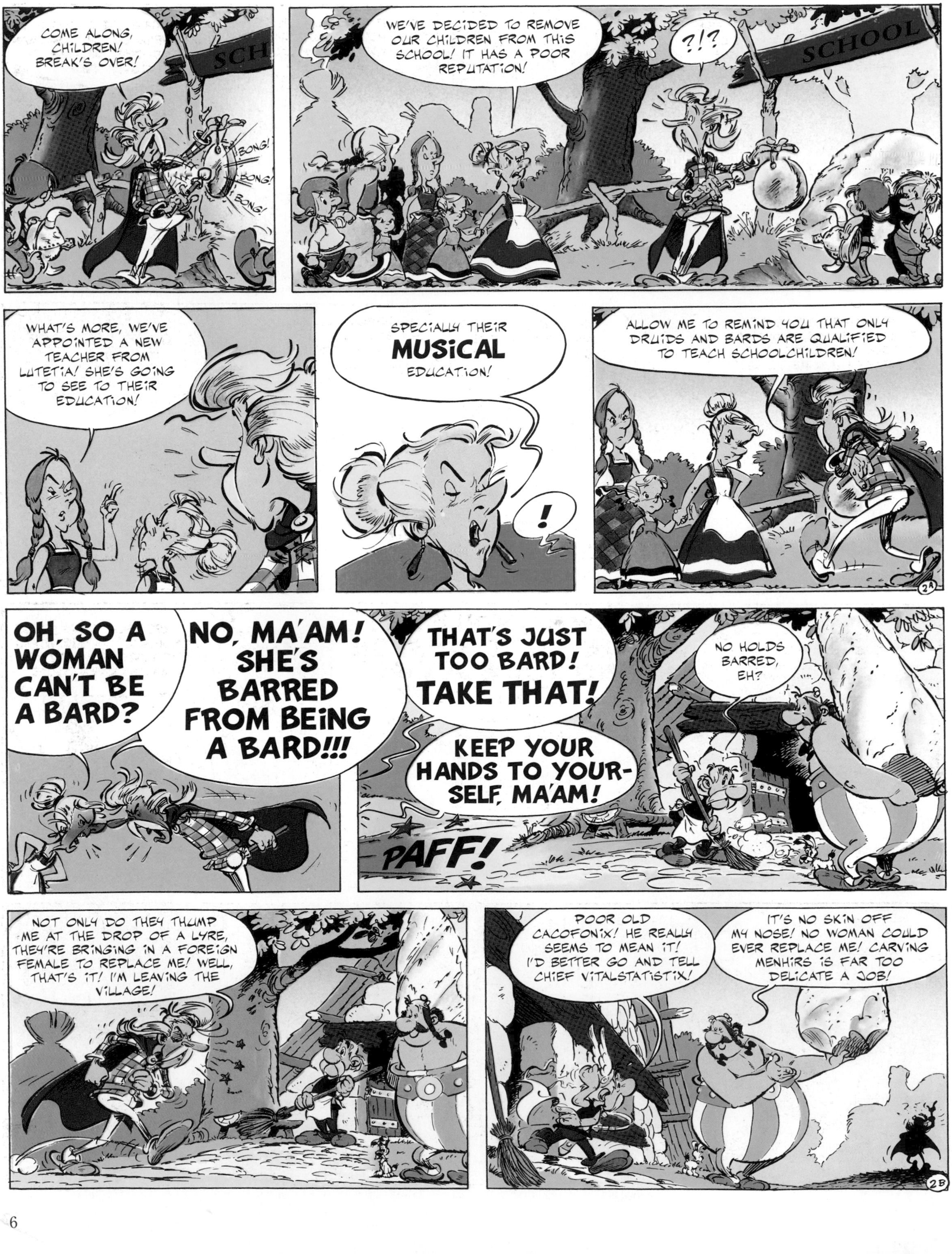
COME ALONG, CHILDREN! BREAK'S OVER!
SCH
BONG!
BONG!
BONG!
WE'VE DECIDED TO REMOVE OUR CHILDREN FROM THIS SCHOOL! IT HAS A POOR REPUTATION!
?!?
SCHOOL
WHAT'S MORE, WE'VE APPOINTED A NEW TEACHER FROM LUTETIA! SHE'S GOING TO SEE TO THEIR EDUCATION!
SPECIALLY THEIR MUSICAL EDUCATION!
!
ALLOW ME TO REMIND YOU THAT ONLY DRUIDS AND BARDS ARE QUALIFIED TO TEACH SCHOOLCHILDREN!
OH, SO A WOMAN CAN'T BE A BARD?
NO, MA'AM! SHE'S BARRED FROM BEING A BARD!!!
THAT'S JUST TOO BARD! TAKE THAT!
KEEP YOUR HANDS TO YOURSELF, MA'AM!
PAFF!
NO HOLDS BARRED, EH?
NOT ONLY DO THEY THUMP ME AT THE DROP OF A LYRE, THEY'RE BRINGING IN A FOREIGN FEMALE TO REPLACE ME! WELL, THAT'S IT! I'M LEAVING THE VILLAGE!
POOR OLD CACOFONIX! HE REALLY SEEMS TO MEAN IT! I'D BETTER GO AND TELL CHIEF VITALSTATISTIX!
IT'S NO SKIN OFF MY NOSE! NO WOMAN COULD EVER REPLACE ME! CARVING MENHIRS IS FAR TOO DELICATE A JOB!

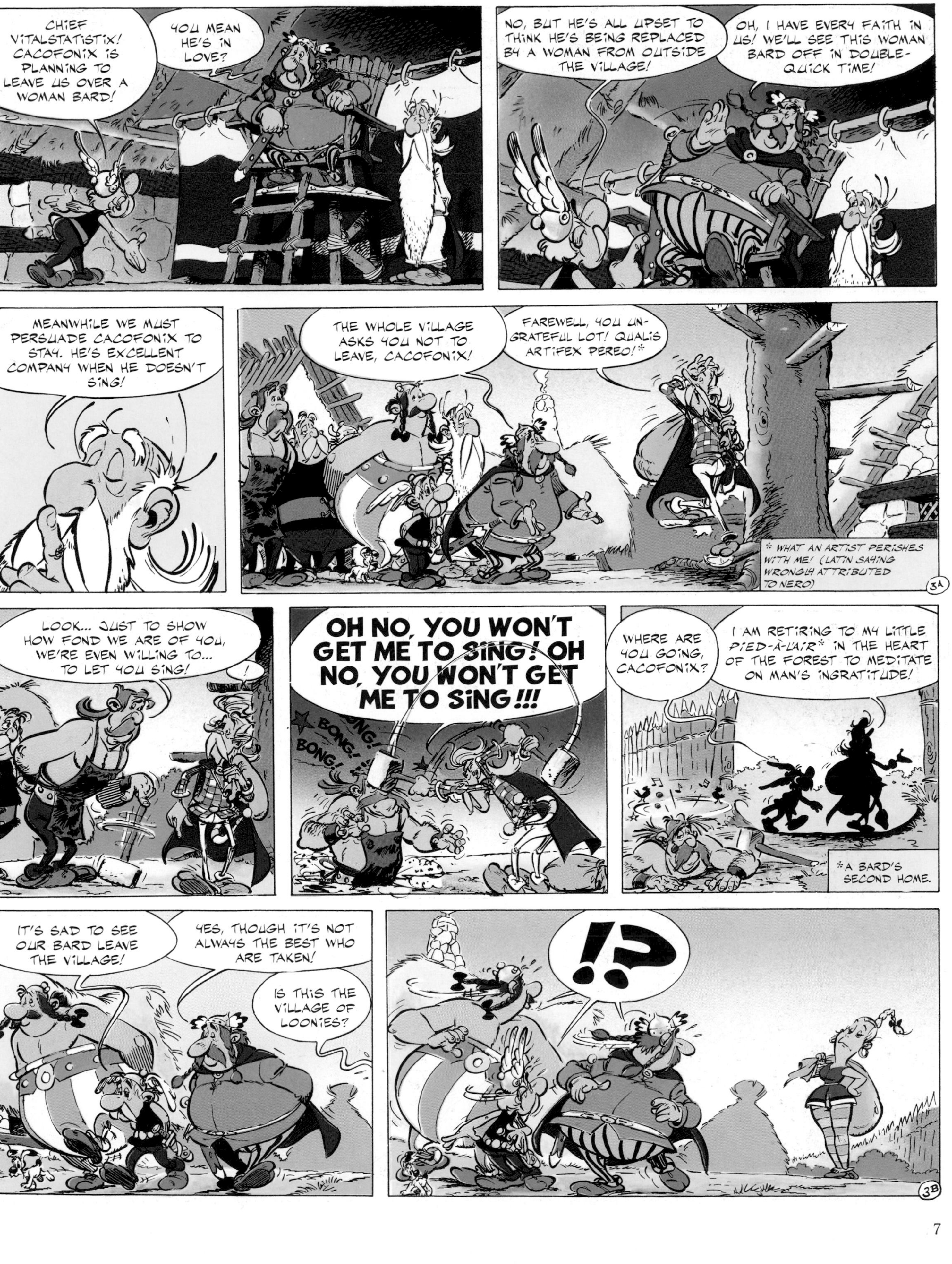
CHIEF VITALSTATISTIX! CACOFONIX IS PLANNING TO LEAVE US OVER A WOMAN BARD!
YOU MEAN HE'S IN LOVE?
NO, BUT HE'S ALL UPSET TO THINK HE'S BEING REPLACED BY A WOMAN FROM OUTSIDE THE VILLAGE!
OH, I HAVE EVERY FAITH IN US! WE'LL SEE THIS WOMAN BARD OFF IN DOUBLE-QUICK TIME!
MEANWHILE WE MUST PERSUADE CACOFONIX TO STAY. HE'S EXCELLENT COMPANY WHEN HE DOESN'T SING!
THE WHOLE VILLAGE ASKS YOU NOT TO LEAVE, CACOFONIX!
FAREWELL, YOU UNGRATEFUL LOT! QUALIS ARTIFEX PEREO!*
* WHAT AN ARTIST PERISHES WITH ME! (LATIN SAYING WRONGLY ATTRIBUTED TO NERO)
LOOK... JUST TO SHOW HOW FOND WE ARE OF YOU, WE'RE EVEN WILLING TO... TO LET YOU SING!
!
OH NO, YOU WON'T GET ME TO SING! OH NO, YOU WON'T GET ME TO SING!!!
BONG! BONG!
WHERE ARE YOU GOING, CACOFONIX?
I AM RETIRING TO MY LITTLE PIED-À-LAIR* IN THE HEART OF THE FOREST TO MEDITATE ON MAN'S INGRATITUDE!
*A BARD'S SECOND HOME.
IT'S SAD TO SEE OUR BARD LEAVE THE VILLAGE!
YES, THOUGH IT'S NOT ALWAYS THE BEST WHO ARE TAKEN!
IS THIS THE VILLAGE OF LOONIES?
!?

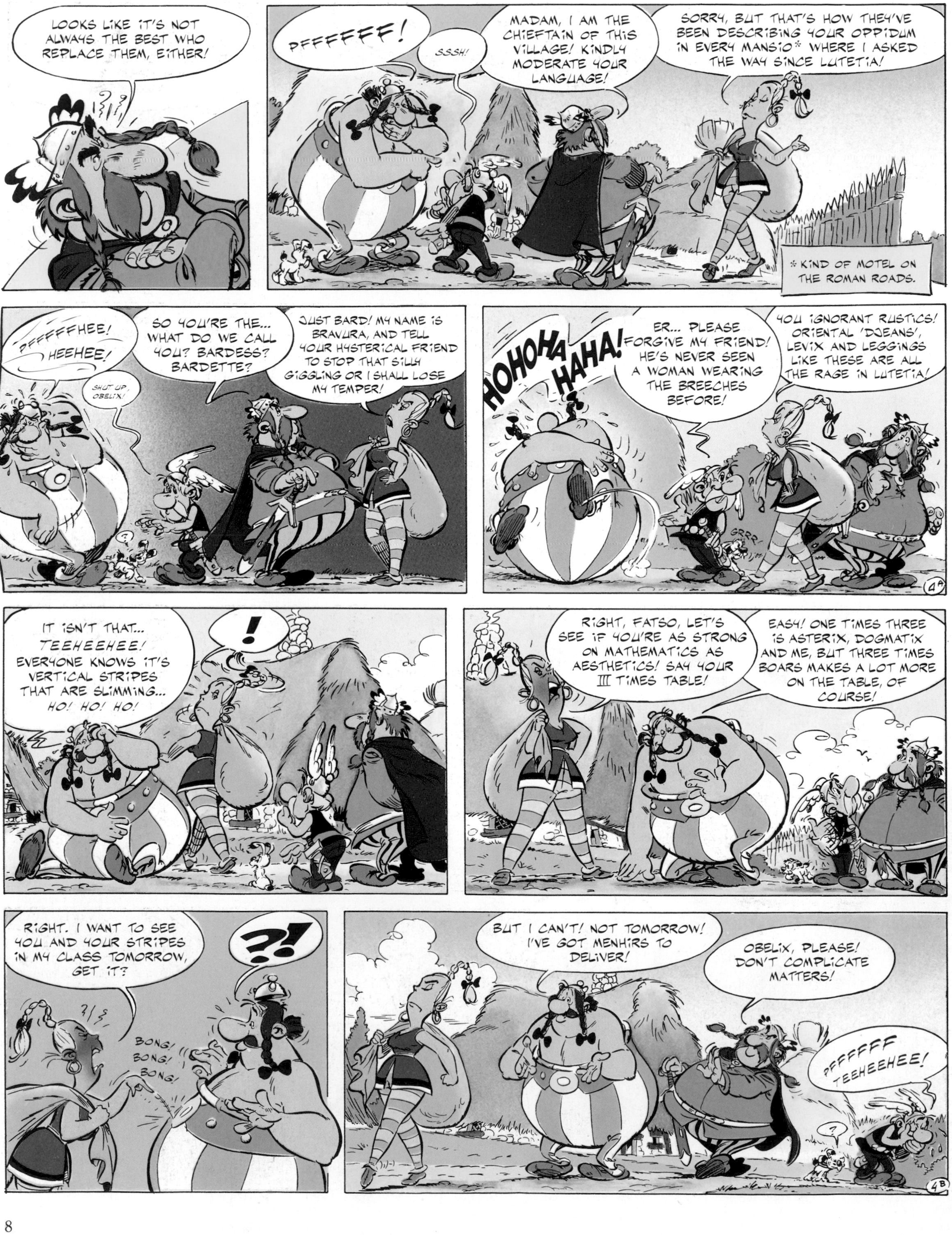
LOOKS LIKE IT'S NOT ALWAYS THE BEST WHO REPLACE THEM, EITHER!
PFFFFFF!
SSSH!
MADAM, I AM THE CHIEFTAIN OF THIS VILLAGE! KINDLY MODERATE YOUR LANGUAGE!
SORRY, BUT THAT'S HOW THEY'VE BEEN DESCRIBING YOUR OPPIDUM IN EVERY MANSIO* WHERE I ASKED THE WAY SINCE LUTETIA!
* KIND OF MOTEL ON THE ROMAN ROADS.
PFFFFFHEE! HEEHEE!
SHUT UP, OBELIX!
SO YOU'RE THE... WHAT DO WE CALL YOU? BARDESS? BARDETTE?
JUST BARD! MY NAME IS BRAVURA, AND TELL YOUR HYSTERICAL FRIEND TO STOP THAT SILLY GIGGLING OR I SHALL LOSE MY TEMPER!
HOHOHA HAHA!
ER... PLEASE FORGIVE MY FRIEND! HE'S NEVER SEEN A WOMAN WEARING THE BREECHES BEFORE!
YOU IGNORANT RUSTICS! ORIENTAL 'DJEANS', LEVIX AND LEGGINGS LIKE THESE ARE ALL THE RAGE IN LUTETIA!
GRRR!
IT ISN'T THAT... TEEHEEHEE! EVERYONE KNOWS IT'S VERTICAL STRIPES THAT ARE SLIMMING... HO! HO! HO!
!
RIGHT, FATSO, LET'S SEE IF YOU'RE AS STRONG ON MATHEMATICS AS AESTHETICS! SAY YOUR III TIMES TABLE!
EASY! ONE TIMES THREE IS ASTERIX, DOGMATIX AND ME, BUT THREE TIMES BOARS MAKES A LOT MORE ON THE TABLE, OF COURSE!
RIGHT. I WANT TO SEE YOU AND YOUR STRIPES IN MY CLASS TOMORROW, GET IT?
?!
BONG! BONG! BONG!
BUT I CAN'T! NOT TOMORROW! I'VE GOT MENHIRS TO DELIVER!
OBELIX, PLEASE! DON'T COMPLICATE MATTERS!
PFFFFFF TEEHEEHEE!

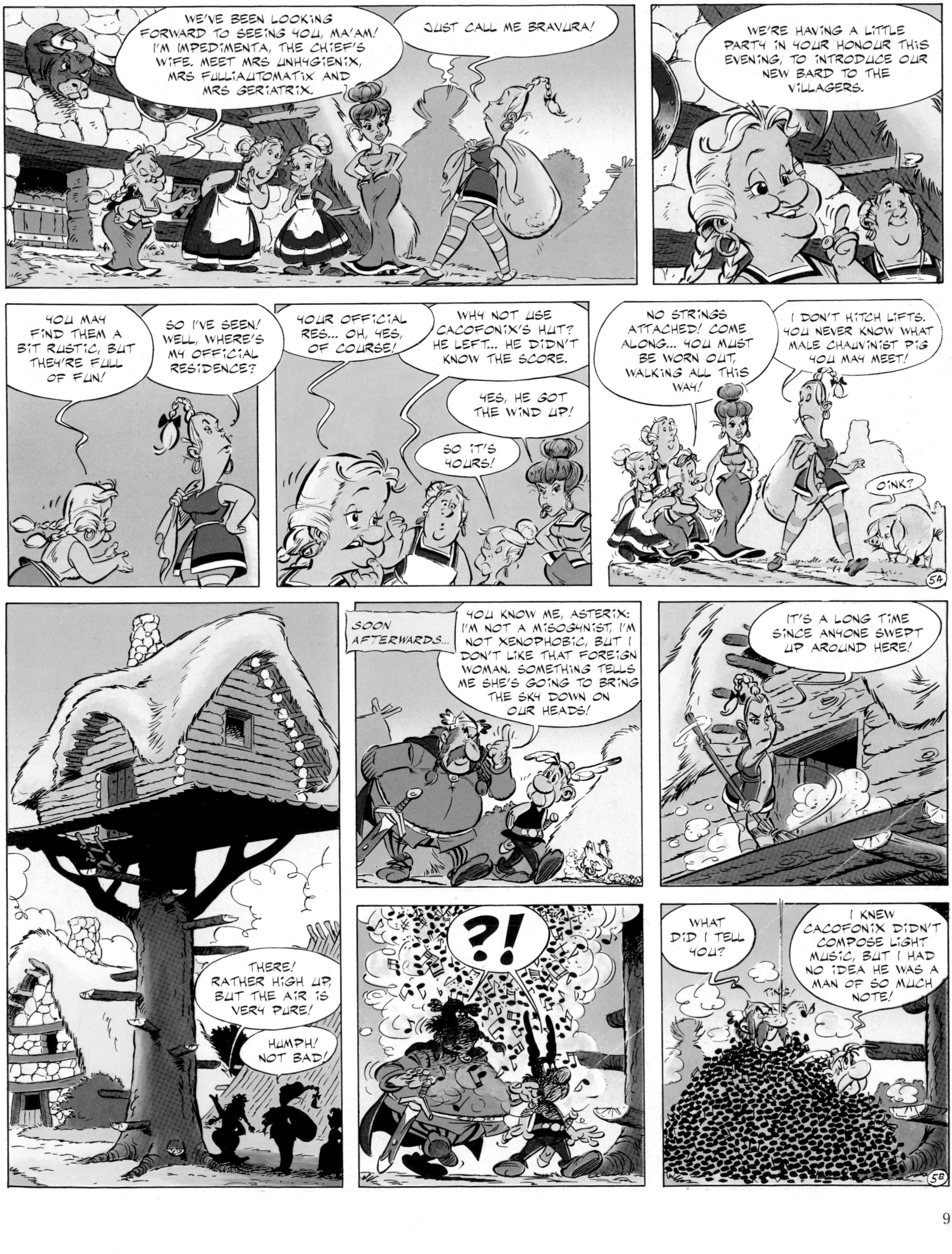
WE'VE BEEN LOOKING FORWARD TO SEEING YOU, MA'AM! I'M IMPEDIMENTA, THE CHIEF'S WIFE. MEET MRS UNHYGIENIX, MRS FULLIAUTOMATIX AND MRS GERIATRIX.
JUST CALL ME BRAVURA!
WE'RE HAVING A LITTLE PARTY IN YOUR HONOUR THIS EVENING, TO INTRODUCE OUR NEW BARD TO THE VILLAGERS.
YOU MAY FIND THEM A BIT RUSTIC, BUT THEY'RE FULL OF FUN!
SO I'VE SEEN! WELL, WHERE'S MY OFFICIAL RESIDENCE?
YOUR OFFICIAL RES... OH, YES, OF COURSE!
WHY NOT USE CACOFONIX'S HUT? HE LEFT... HE DIDN'T KNOW THE SCORE.
YES, HE GOT THE WIND UP!
SO IT'S YOURS!
NO STRINGS ATTACHED! COME ALONG... YOU MUST BE WORN OUT, WALKING ALL THIS WAY!
I DON'T HITCH LIFTS. YOU NEVER KNOW WHAT MALE CHAUVINIST PIG YOU MAY MEET!
OINK?
54
THERE! RATHER HIGH UP, BUT THE AIR IS VERY PURE!
HUMPH! NOT BAD!
SOON AFTERWARDS...
YOU KNOW ME, ASTERIX: I'M NOT A MISOGNYNIST, I'M NOT XENOPHOBIC, BUT I DON'T LIKE THAT FOREIGN WOMAN. SOMETHING TELLS ME SHE'S GOING TO BRING THE SKY DOWN ON OUR HEADS!
IT'S A LONG TIME SINCE ANYONE SWEPT UP AROUND HERE!
?!
WHAT DID I TELL YOU?
I KNEW CACOFONIX DIDN'T COMPOSE LIGHT MUSIC, BUT I HAD NO IDEA HE WAS A MAN OF SO MUCH NOTE!
TING!
58

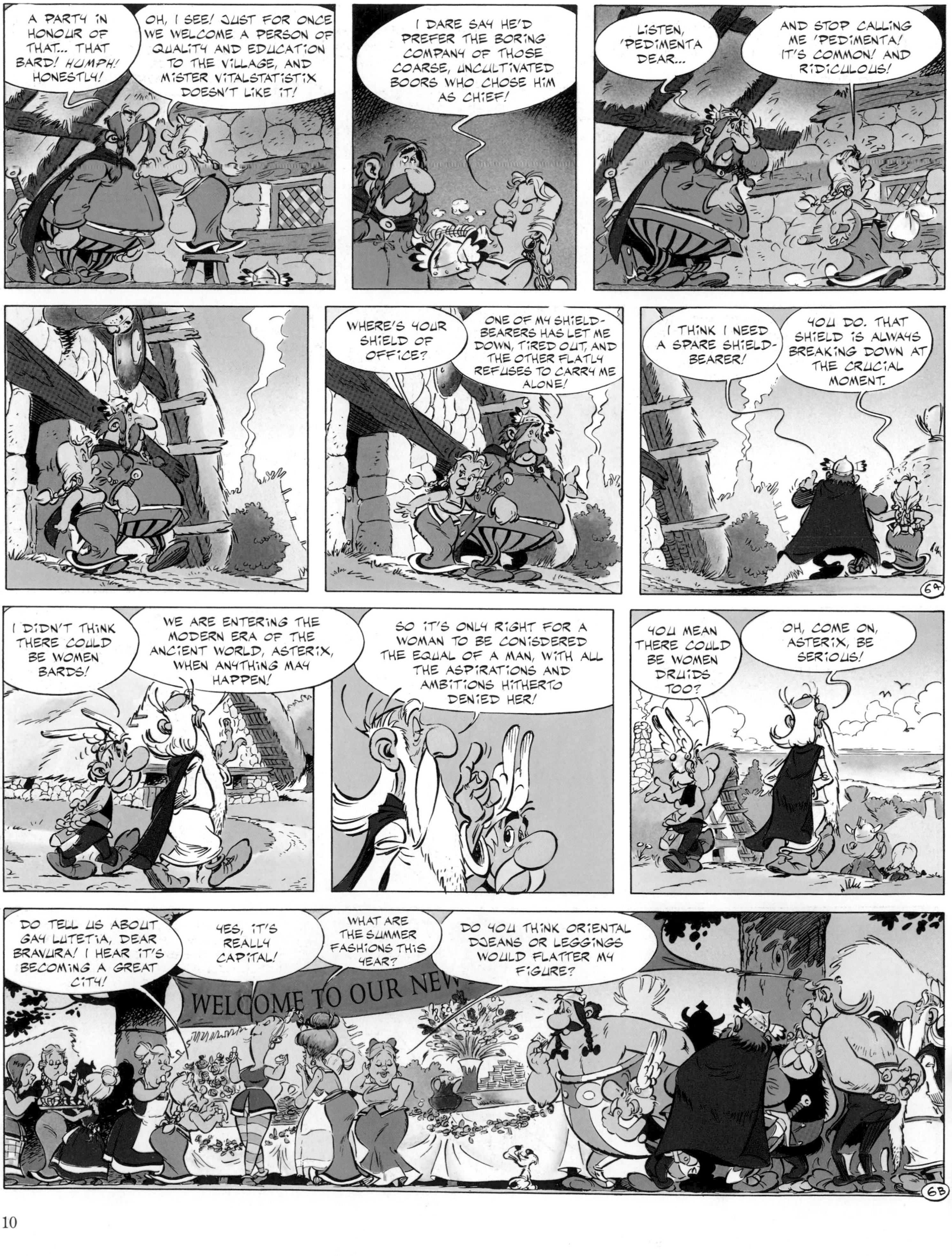

A PARTY IN HONOUR OF THAT... THAT BARD! HUMPH! HONESTLY!
OH, I SEE! JUST FOR ONCE WE WELCOME A PERSON OF QUALITY AND EDUCATION TO THE VILLAGE, AND MISTER VITALSTATISTIX DOESN'T LIKE IT!
I DARE SAY HE'D PREFER THE BORING COMPANY OF THOSE COARSE, UNCULTIVATED BOORS WHO CHOSE HIM AS CHIEF!
LISTEN, 'PEDIMENTA DEAR...
AND STOP CALLING ME 'PEDIMENTA! IT'S COMMON! AND RIDICULOUS!
WHERE'S YOUR SHIELD OF OFFICE?
ONE OF MY SHIELD-BEARERS HAS LET ME DOWN, TIRED OUT, AND THE OTHER FLATLY REFUSES TO CARRY ME ALONE!
I THINK I NEED A SPARE SHIELD-BEARER!
YOU DO. THAT SHIELD IS ALWAYS BREAKING DOWN AT THE CRUCIAL MOMENT.
I DIDN'T THINK THERE COULD BE WOMEN BARDS!
WE ARE ENTERING THE MODERN ERA OF THE ANCIENT WORLD, ASTERIX, WHEN ANYTHING MAY HAPPEN!
SO IT'S ONLY RIGHT FOR A WOMAN TO BE CONISDERED THE EQUAL OF A MAN, WITH ALL THE ASPIRATIONS AND AMBITIONS HITHERTO DENIED HER!
YOU MEAN THERE COULD BE WOMEN DRUIDS TOO?
OH, COME ON, ASTERIX, BE SERIOUS!
DO TELL US ABOUT GAY LUTETIA, DEAR BRAVURA! I HEAR IT'S BECOMING A GREAT CITY!
YES, IT'S REALLY CAPITAL!
WHAT ARE THE SUMMER FASHIONS THIS YEAR?
DO YOU THINK ORIENTAL DJEANS OR LEGGINGS WOULD FLATTER MY FIGURE?
WELCOME TO OUR NEW

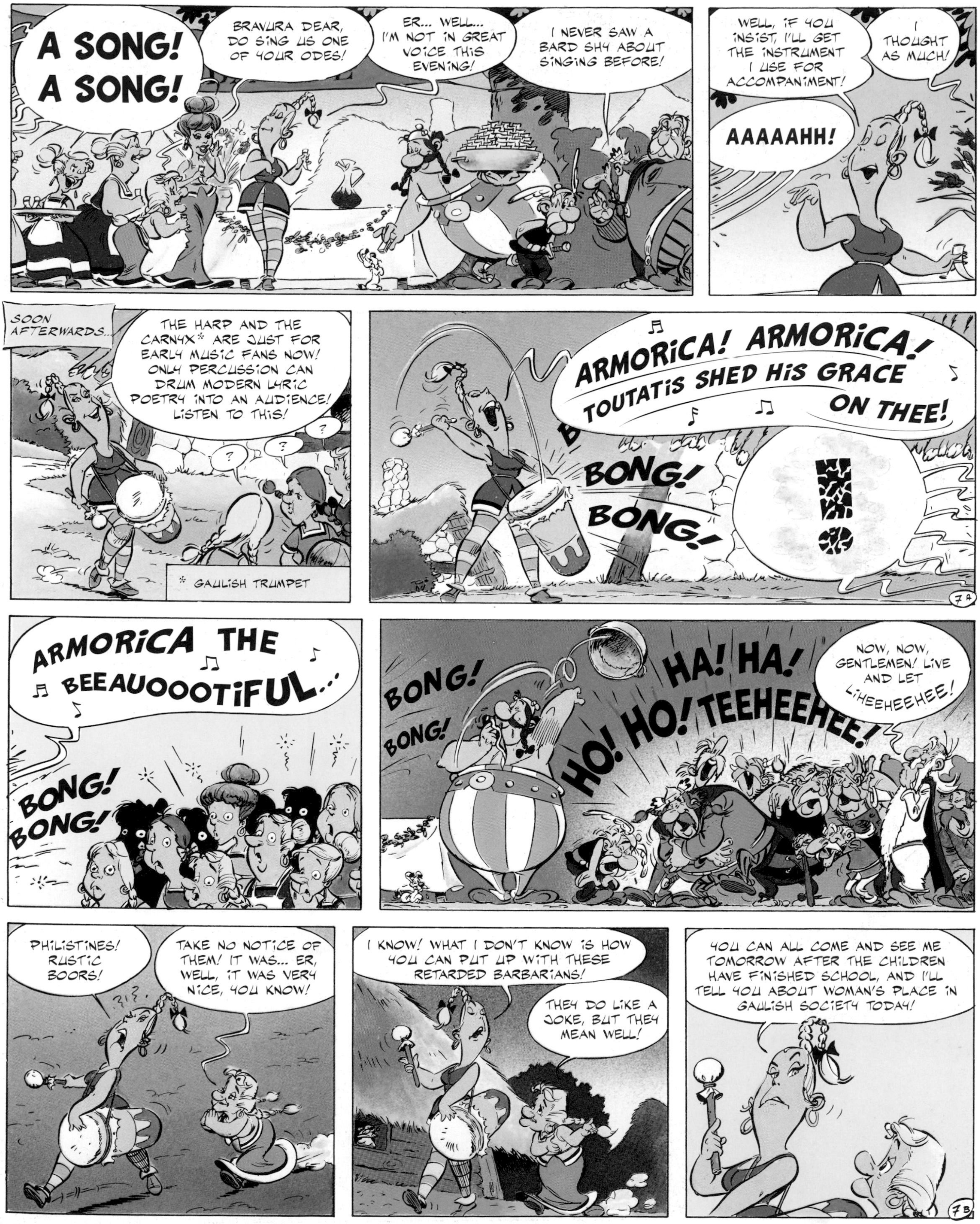

A SONG! A SONG!
BRAVURA DEAR, DO SING US ONE OF YOUR ODES!
ER... WELL... I'M NOT IN GREAT VOICE THIS EVENING!
I NEVER SAW A BARD SHY ABOUT SINGING BEFORE!
WELL, IF YOU INSIST, I'LL GET THE INSTRUMENT I USE FOR ACCOMPANIMENT!
I THOUGHT AS MUCH!
AAAAAHH!
SOON AFTERWARDS...
THE HARP AND THE CARNYX* ARE JUST FOR EARLY MUSIC FANS NOW! ONLY PERCUSSION CAN DRUM MODERN LYRIC POETRY INTO AN AUDIENCE! LISTEN TO THIS!
?
?
?
* GAULISH TRUMPET
ARMORICA! ARMORICA! TOUTATIS SHED HIS GRACE ON THEE!
BONG!
BONG!
!
ARMORICA THE BEEAUOOOTIFUL...
BONG!
BONG!
BONG!
BONG!
HA! HA!
HO! HO! TEEHEEHEE!
NOW, NOW, GENTLEMEN! LIVE AND LET LIHEEHEEHEE!
PHILISTINES! RUSTIC BOORS!
TAKE NO NOTICE OF THEM! IT WAS... ER, WELL, IT WAS VERY NICE, YOU KNOW!
I KNOW! WHAT I DON'T KNOW IS HOW YOU CAN PUT UP WITH THESE RETARDED BARBARIANS!
THEY DO LIKE A JOKE, BUT THEY MEAN WELL!
YOU CAN ALL COME AND SEE ME TOMORROW AFTER THE CHILDREN HAVE FINISHED SCHOOL, AND I'LL TELL YOU ABOUT WOMAN'S PLACE IN GAULISH SOCIETY TODAY!

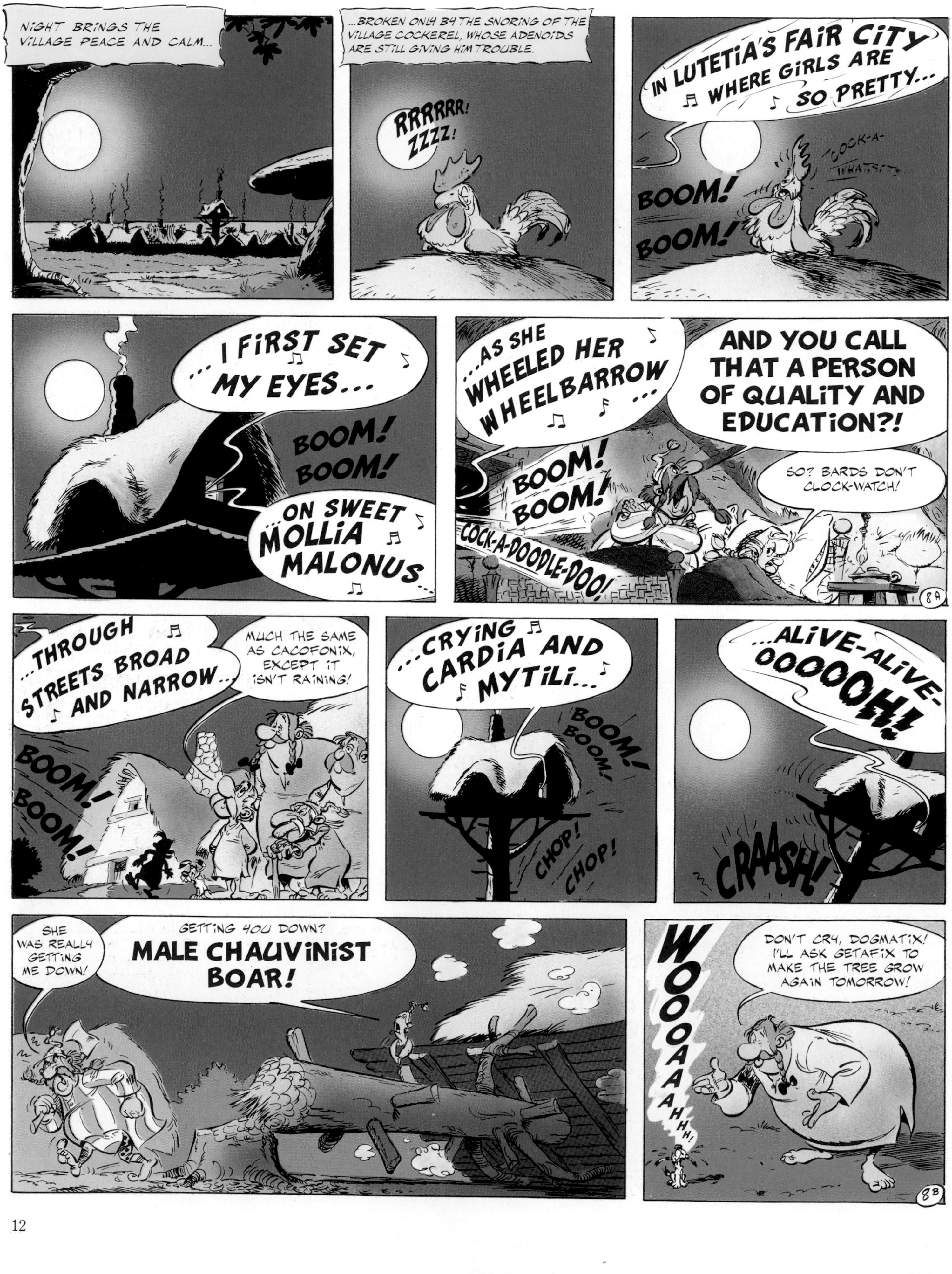
NIGHT BRINGS THE VILLAGE PEACE AND CALM...
...BROKEN ONLY BY THE SNORING OF THE VILLAGE COCKEREL, WHOSE ADENOIDS ARE STILL GIVING HIM TROUBLE.
RRRRRR! ZZZZ!
IN LUTETIA'S FAIR CITY WHERE GIRLS ARE SO PRETTY...
COCK-A-
WHATSIT!
BOOM!
BOOM!
...I FIRST SET MY EYES...
BOOM! BOOM!
...ON SWEET MOLLIA MALONUS...
...AS SHE WHEELED HER WHEELBARROW...
AND YOU CALL THAT A PERSON OF QUALITY AND EDUCATION?!
BOOM! BOOM!
SO? BARDS DON'T CLOCK-WATCH!
COCK-A-DOODLE-DOO!
8A
...THROUGH STREETS BROAD AND NARROW...
MUCH THE SAME AS CACOFONIX, EXCEPT IT ISN'T RAINING!
BOOM! BOOM!
...CRYING CARDIA AND MYTILI...
BOOM! BOOM!
CHOP! CHOP!
...ALIVE-ALIVE-OOOOOOH!!
CRAASH!
SHE WAS REALLY GETTING ME DOWN!
GETTING YOU DOWN?
MALE CHAUVINIST BOAR!
WOOOAAAHHH!
DON'T CRY, DOGMATIX! I'LL ASK GETAFIX TO MAKE THE TREE GROW AGAIN TOMORROW!
8B

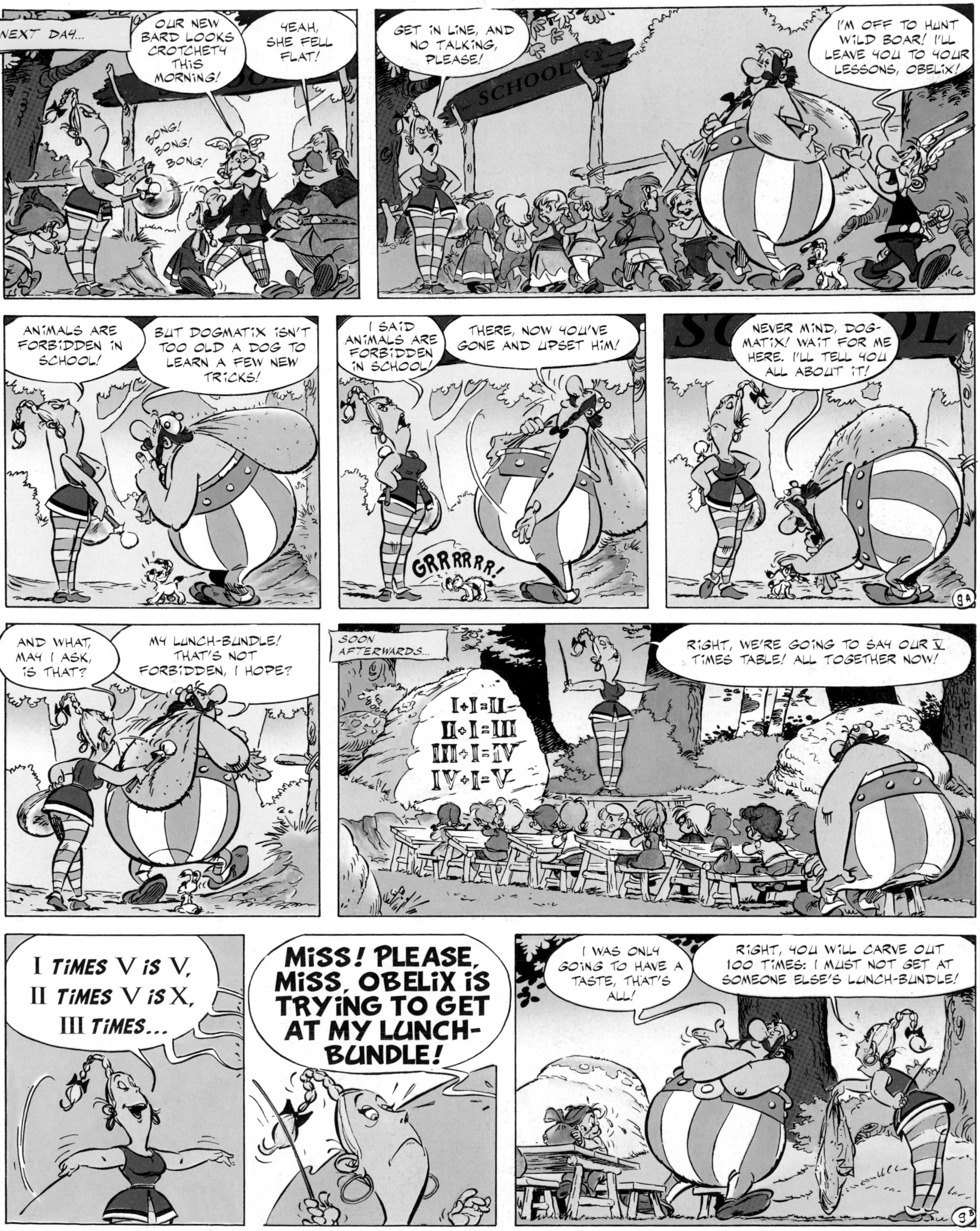
NEXT DAY...
OUR NEW BARD LOOKS CROTCHETY THIS MORNING!
YEAH, SHE FELL FLAT!
BONG! BONG! BONG!
SCHOOL
GET IN LINE, AND NO TALKING, PLEASE!
I'M OFF TO HUNT WILD BOAR! I'LL LEAVE YOU TO YOUR LESSONS, OBELIX!
ANIMALS ARE FORBIDDEN IN SCHOOL!
BUT DOGMATIX ISN'T TOO OLD A DOG TO LEARN A FEW NEW TRICKS!
I SAID ANIMALS ARE FORBIDDEN IN SCHOOL!
THERE, NOW YOU'VE GONE AND UPSET HIM!
GRRRRRR!
NEVER MIND, DOGMATIX! WAIT FOR ME HERE. I'LL TELL YOU ALL ABOUT IT!
AND WHAT, MAY I ASK, IS THAT?
MY LUNCH-BUNDLE! THAT'S NOT FORBIDDEN, I HOPE?
SOON AFTERWARDS...
I+I=II
II+I=III
III+I=IV
IV+I=V
RIGHT, WE'RE GOING TO SAY OUR V TIMES TABLE! ALL TOGETHER NOW!
I TIMES V IS V, II TIMES V IS X, III TIMES...
MISS! PLEASE, MISS, OBELIX IS TRYING TO GET AT MY LUNCH-BUNDLE!
I WAS ONLY GOING TO HAVE A TASTE, THAT'S ALL!
RIGHT, YOU WILL CARVE OUT 100 TIMES: I MUST NOT GET AT SOMEONE ELSE'S LUNCH-BUNDLE!

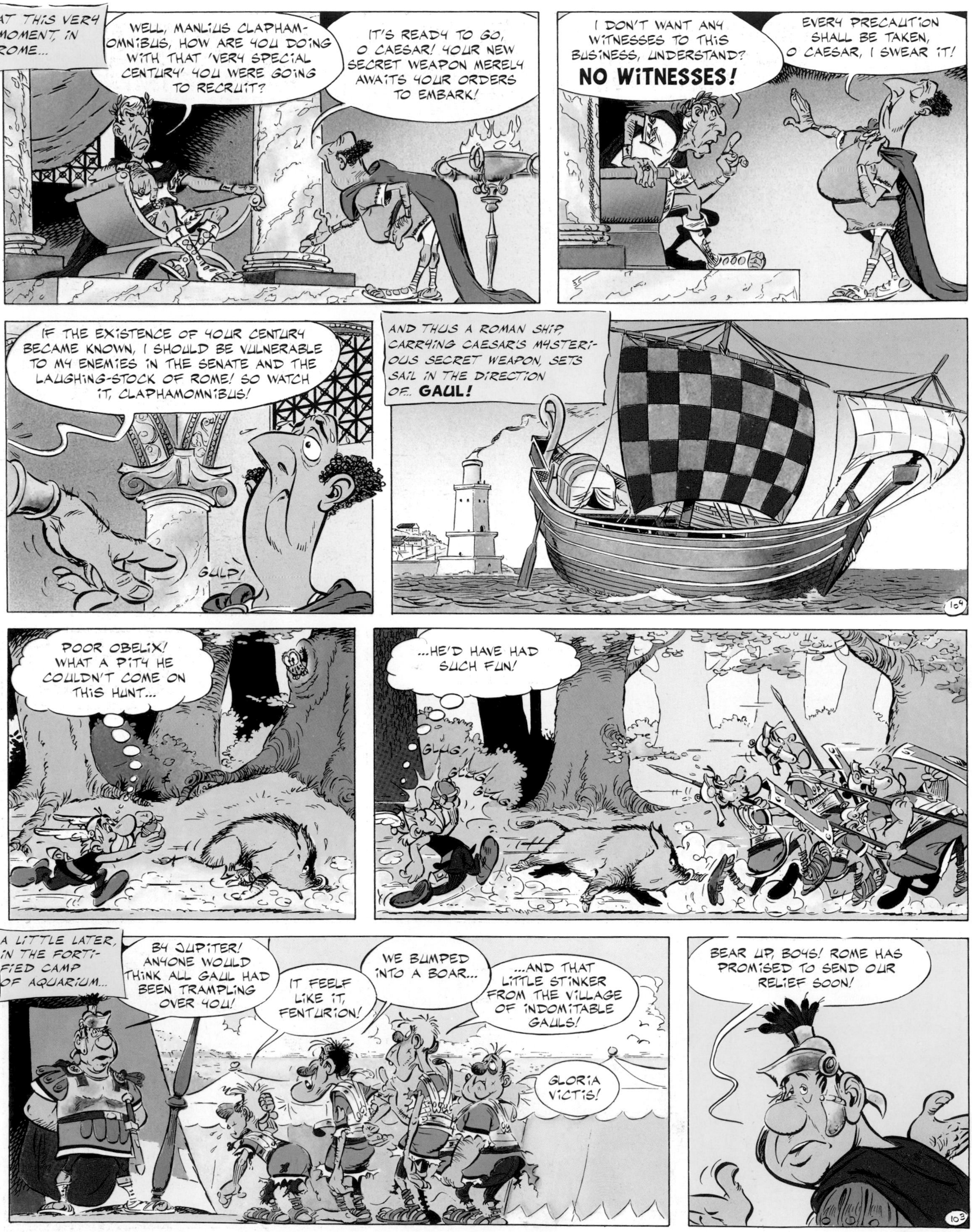
AT THIS VERY MOMENT, IN ROME...
WELL, MANLIUS CLAPHAMOMNIBUS, HOW ARE YOU DOING WITH THAT 'VERY SPECIAL CENTURY' YOU WERE GOING TO RECRUIT?
IT'S READY TO GO, O CAESAR! YOUR NEW SECRET WEAPON MERELY AWAITS YOUR ORDERS TO EMBARK!
I DON'T WANT ANY WITNESSES TO THIS BUSINESS, UNDERSTAND? NO WITNESSES!
EVERY PRECAUTION SHALL BE TAKEN, O CAESAR, I SWEAR IT!
IF THE EXISTENCE OF YOUR CENTURY BECAME KNOWN, I SHOULD BE VULNERABLE TO MY ENEMIES IN THE SENATE AND THE LAUGHING-STOCK OF ROME! SO WATCH IT, CLAPHAMOMNIBUS!
GULP!
AND THUS A ROMAN SHIP, CARRYING CAESAR'S MYSTERIOUS SECRET WEAPON, SETS SAIL IN THE DIRECTION OF... GAUL!
POOR OBELIX! WHAT A PITY HE COULDN'T COME ON THIS HUNT...
...HE'D HAVE HAD SUCH FUN!
GLUG! GLUG! GLUG!
A LITTLE LATER, IN THE FORTIFIED CAMP OF AQUARIUM...
BY JUPITER! ANYONE WOULD THINK ALL GAUL HAD BEEN TRAMPLING OVER YOU!
IT FEELF LIKE IT, FENTURION!
WE BUMPED INTO A BOAR...
...AND THAT LITTLE STINKER FROM THE VILLAGE OF INDOMITABLE GAULS!
GLORIA VICTIS!
BEAR UP, BOYS! ROME HAS PROMISED TO SEND OUR RELIEF SOON!

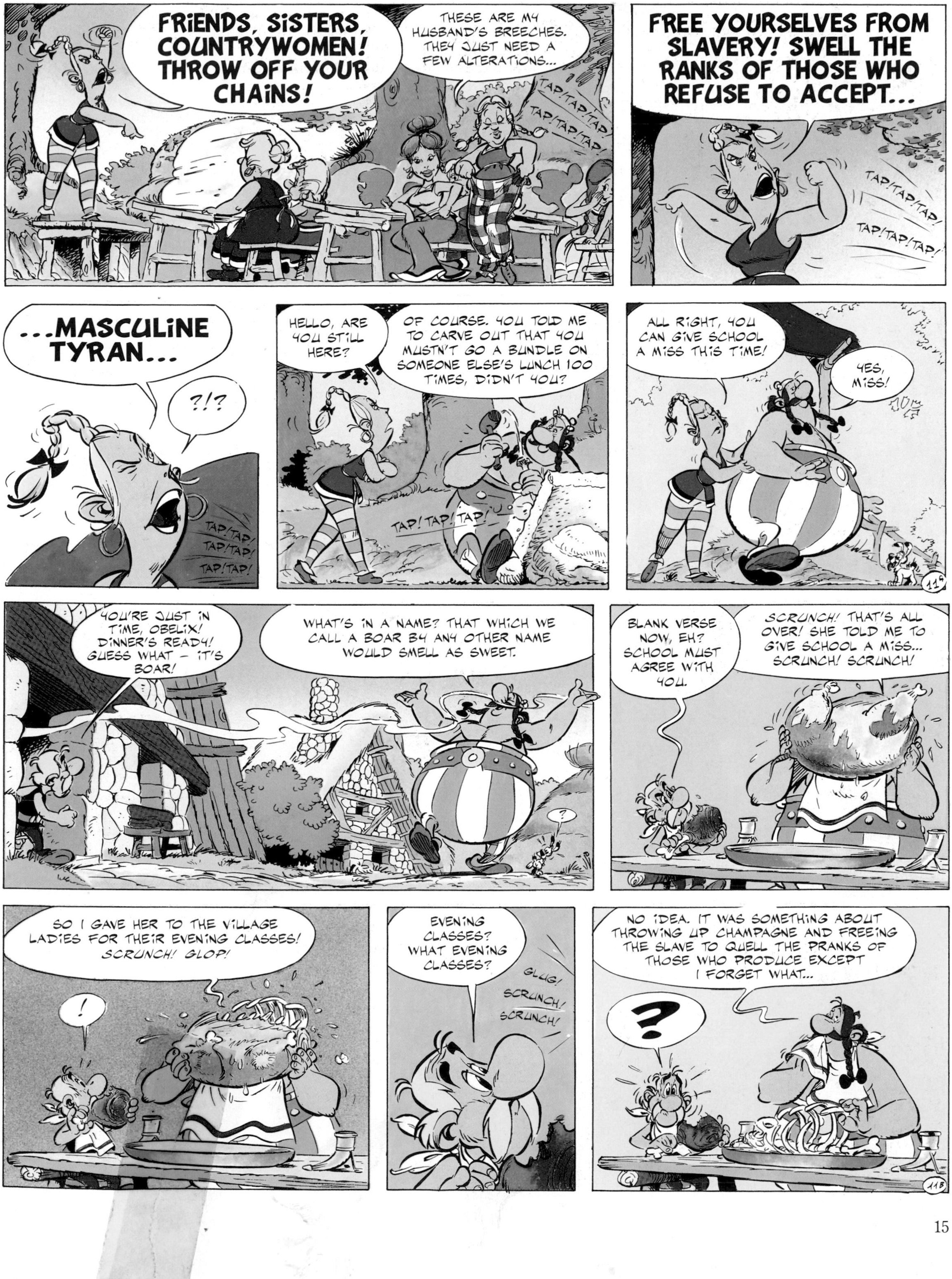
FRIENDS, SISTERS, COUNTRYWOMEN! THROW OFF YOUR CHAINS!
THESE ARE MY HUSBAND'S BREECHES. THEY JUST NEED A FEW ALTERATIONS...
TAP! TAP! TAP! TAP! TAP! TAP!
FREE YOURSELVES FROM SLAVERY! SWELL THE RANKS OF THOSE WHO REFUSE TO ACCEPT...
TAP! TAP! TAP! TAP! TAP! TAP!
...MASCULINE TYRAN...
?!?
TAP! TAP! TAP! TAP! TAP! TAP!
HELLO, ARE YOU STILL HERE?
OF COURSE. YOU TOLD ME TO CARVE OUT THAT YOU MUSTN'T GO A BUNDLE ON SOMEONE ELSE'S LUNCH 100 TIMES, DIDN'T YOU?
TAP! TAP! TAP!
ALL RIGHT, YOU CAN GIVE SCHOOL A MISS THIS TIME!
YES, MISS!
YOU'RE JUST IN TIME, OBELIX! DINNER'S READY! GUESS WHAT – IT'S BOAR!
WHAT'S IN A NAME? THAT WHICH WE CALL A BOAR BY ANY OTHER NAME WOULD SMELL AS SWEET.
?
BLANK VERSE NOW, EH? SCHOOL MUST AGREE WITH YOU.
SCRUNCH! THAT'S ALL OVER! SHE TOLD ME TO GIVE SCHOOL A MISS... SCRUNCH! SCRUNCH!
SO I GAVE HER TO THE VILLAGE LADIES FOR THEIR EVENING CLASSES! SCRUNCH! GLOP!
!
EVENING CLASSES? WHAT EVENING CLASSES?
GLUG! SCRUNCH! SCRUNCH!
NO IDEA. IT WAS SOMETHING ABOUT THROWING UP CHAMPAGNE AND FREEING THE SLAVE TO QUELL THE PRANKS OF THOSE WHO PRODUCE EXCEPT I FORGET WHAT...
?

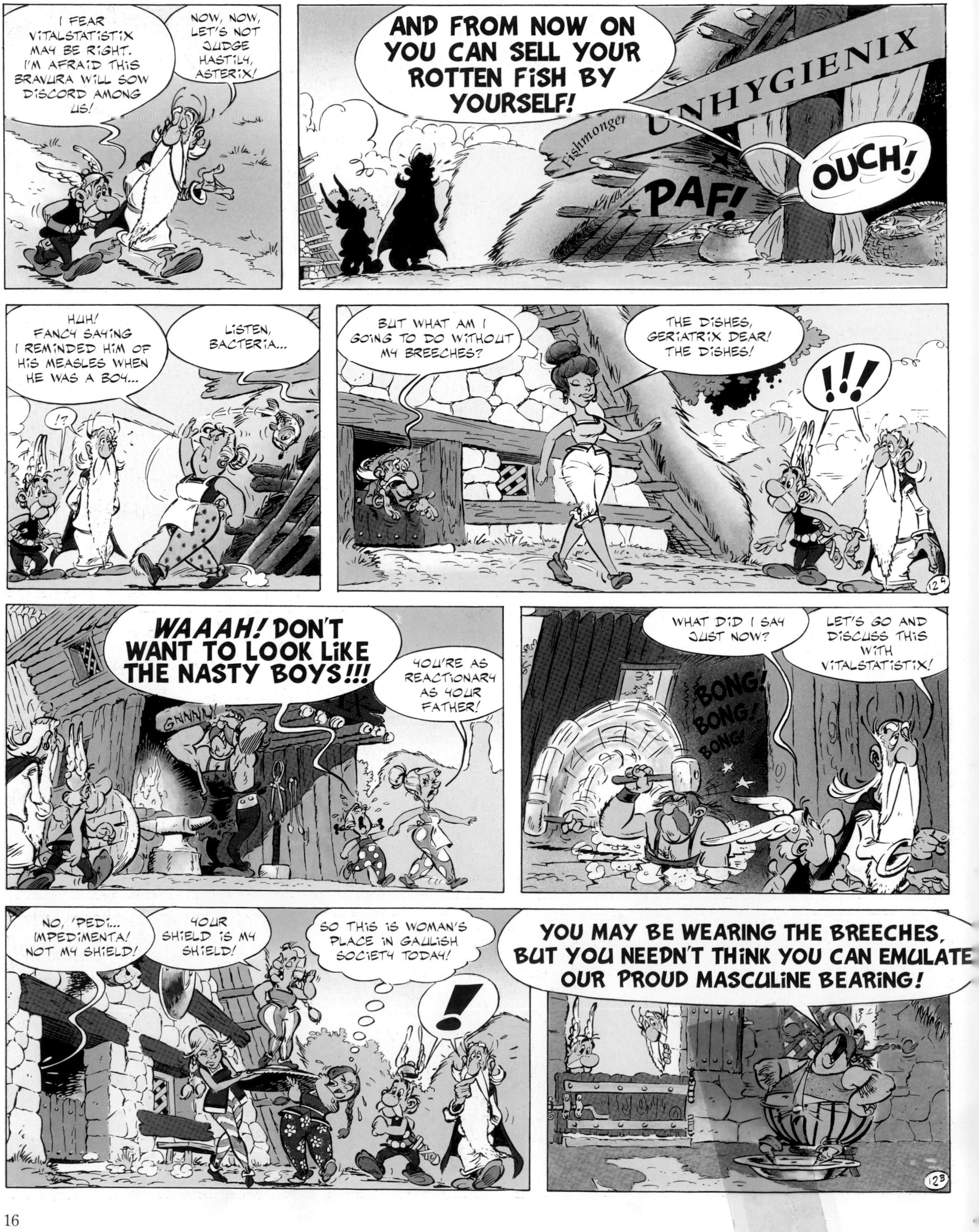
I FEAR VITALSTATISTIX MAY BE RIGHT. I'M AFRAID THIS BRAVURA WILL SOW DISCORD AMONG US!
NOW, NOW, LET'S NOT JUDGE HASTILY, ASTERIX!
AND FROM NOW ON YOU CAN SELL YOUR ROTTEN FISH BY YOURSELF!
UNHYGIENIX
Fishmonger
PAF!
OUCH!
HUH! FANCY SAYING I REMINDED HIM OF HIS MEASLES WHEN HE WAS A BOY...
LISTEN, BACTERIA...
!?
BUT WHAT AM I GOING TO DO WITHOUT MY BREECHES?
THE DISHES, GERIATRIX DEAR! THE DISHES!
!!!
WAAAH! DON'T WANT TO LOOK LIKE THE NASTY BOYS!!!
YOU'RE AS REACTIONARY AS YOUR FATHER!
GNNNN!
WHAT DID I SAY JUST NOW?
LET'S GO AND DISCUSS THIS WITH VITALSTATISTIX!
BONG! BONG! BONG!
NO, 'PEDI... IMPEDIMENTA! NOT MY SHIELD!
YOUR SHIELD IS MY SHIELD!
SO THIS IS WOMAN'S PLACE IN GAULISH SOCIETY TODAY!
!
YOU MAY BE WEARING THE BREECHES, BUT YOU NEEDN'T THINK YOU CAN EMULATE OUR PROUD MASCULINE BEARING!

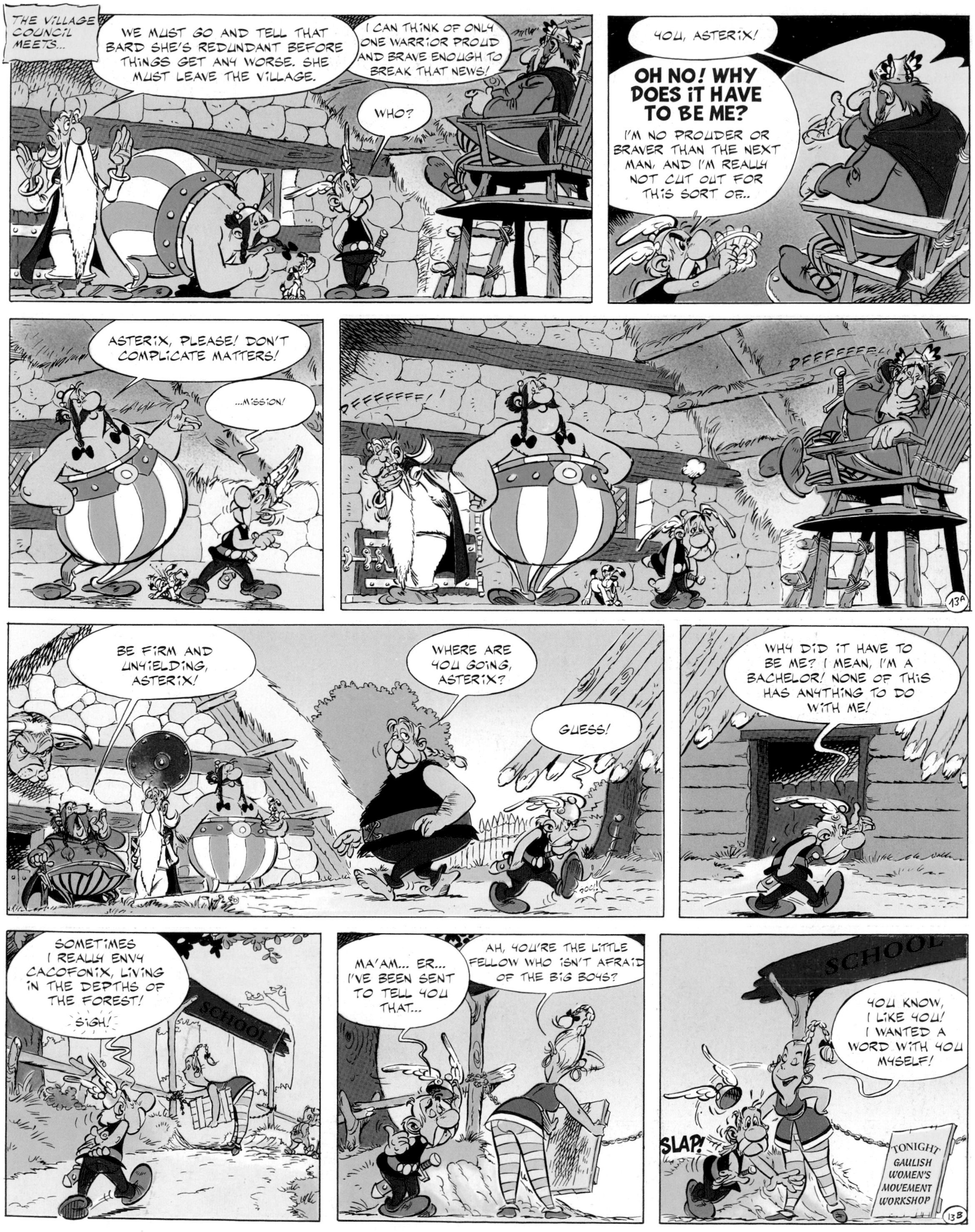

THE VILLAGE COUNCIL MEETS...
WE MUST GO AND TELL THAT BARD SHE'S REDUNDANT BEFORE THINGS GET ANY WORSE. SHE MUST LEAVE THE VILLAGE.
I CAN THINK OF ONLY ONE WARRIOR PROUD AND BRAVE ENOUGH TO BREAK THAT NEWS!
WHO?
YOU, ASTERIX!
OH NO! WHY DOES IT HAVE TO BE ME? I'M NO PROUDER OR BRAVER THAN THE NEXT MAN, AND I'M REALLY NOT CUT OUT FOR THIS SORT OF..
ASTERIX, PLEASE! DON'T COMPLICATE MATTERS!
...MISSION!
PFFFFFFF!
PFFFFFFFF!
13A
BE FIRM AND UNYIELDING, ASTERIX!
WHERE ARE YOU GOING, ASTERIX?
GUESS!
WHY DID IT HAVE TO BE ME? I MEAN, I'M A BACHELOR! NONE OF THIS HAS ANYTHING TO DO WITH ME!
SOMETIMES I REALLY ENVY CACOFONIX, LIVING IN THE DEPTHS OF THE FOREST!
SIGH!
SCHOOL
MA'AM... ER... I'VE BEEN SENT TO TELL YOU THAT...
AH, YOU'RE THE LITTLE FELLOW WHO ISN'T AFRAID OF THE BIG BOYS?
SCHOOL
YOU KNOW, I LIKE YOU! I WANTED A WORD WITH YOU MYSELF!
SLAP!
TONIGHT GAULISH WOMEN'S MOVEMENT WORKSHOP
13B

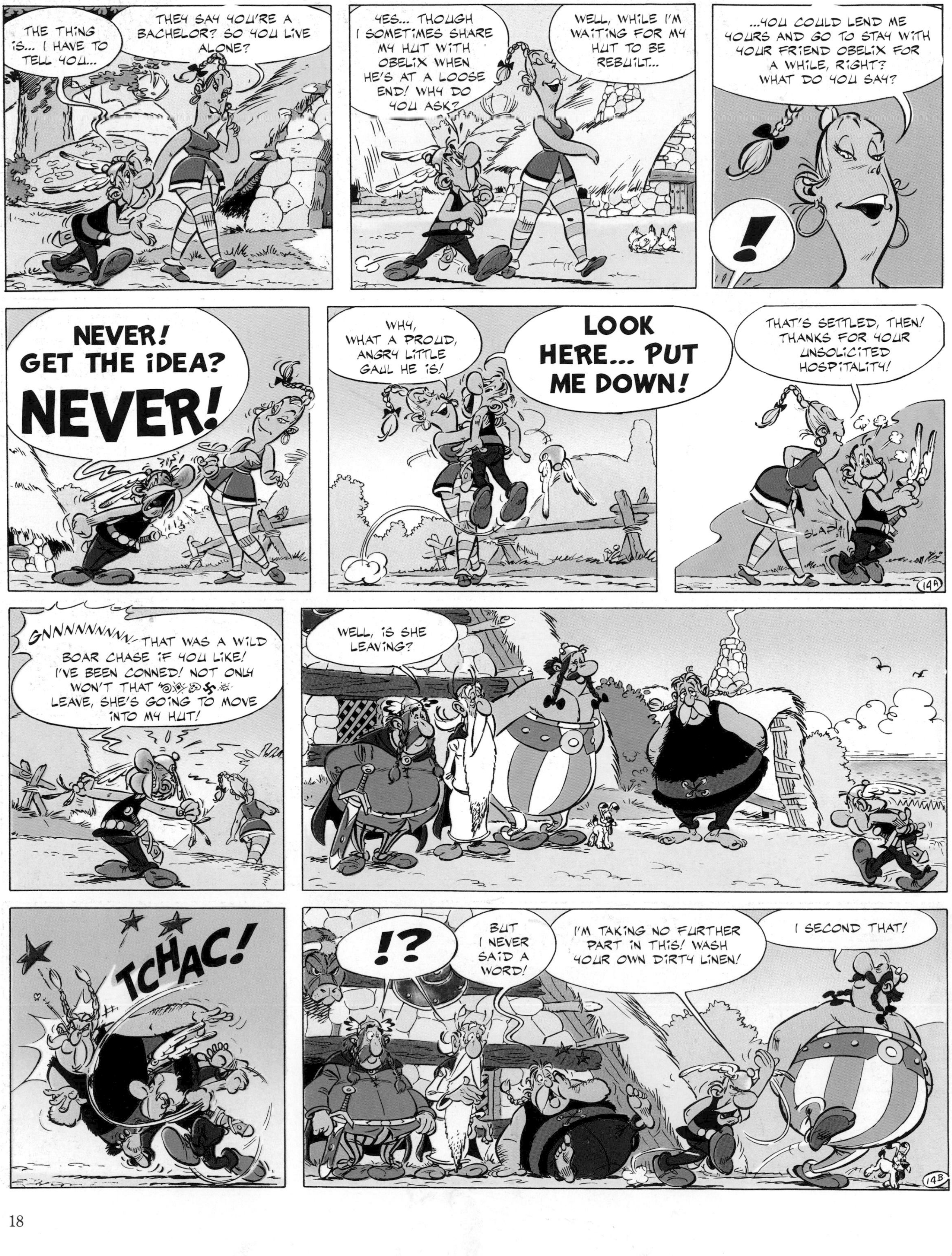
THE THING IS... I HAVE TO TELL YOU...
THEY SAY YOU'RE A BACHELOR? SO YOU LIVE ALONE?
YES... THOUGH I SOMETIMES SHARE MY HUT WITH OBELIX WHEN HE'S AT A LOOSE END! WHY DO YOU ASK?
WELL, WHILE I'M WAITING FOR MY HUT TO BE REBUILT...
...YOU COULD LEND ME YOURS AND GO TO STAY WITH YOUR FRIEND OBELIX FOR A WHILE, RIGHT? WHAT DO YOU SAY?
!
NEVER! GET THE IDEA? NEVER!
WHY, WHAT A PROUD, ANGRY LITTLE GAUL HE IS!
LOOK HERE... PUT ME DOWN!
THAT'S SETTLED, THEN! THANKS FOR YOUR UNSOLICITED HOSPITALITY!
SLAP!
GNNNNNNNN- THAT WAS A WILD BOAR CHASE IF YOU LIKE! I'VE BEEN CONNED! NOT ONLY WON'T THAT LEAVE, SHE'S GOING TO MOVE INTO MY HUT!
WELL, IS SHE LEAVING?
TCHAC!
!?
BUT I NEVER SAID A WORD!
I'M TAKING NO FURTHER PART IN THIS! WASH YOUR OWN DIRTY LINEN!
I SECOND THAT!

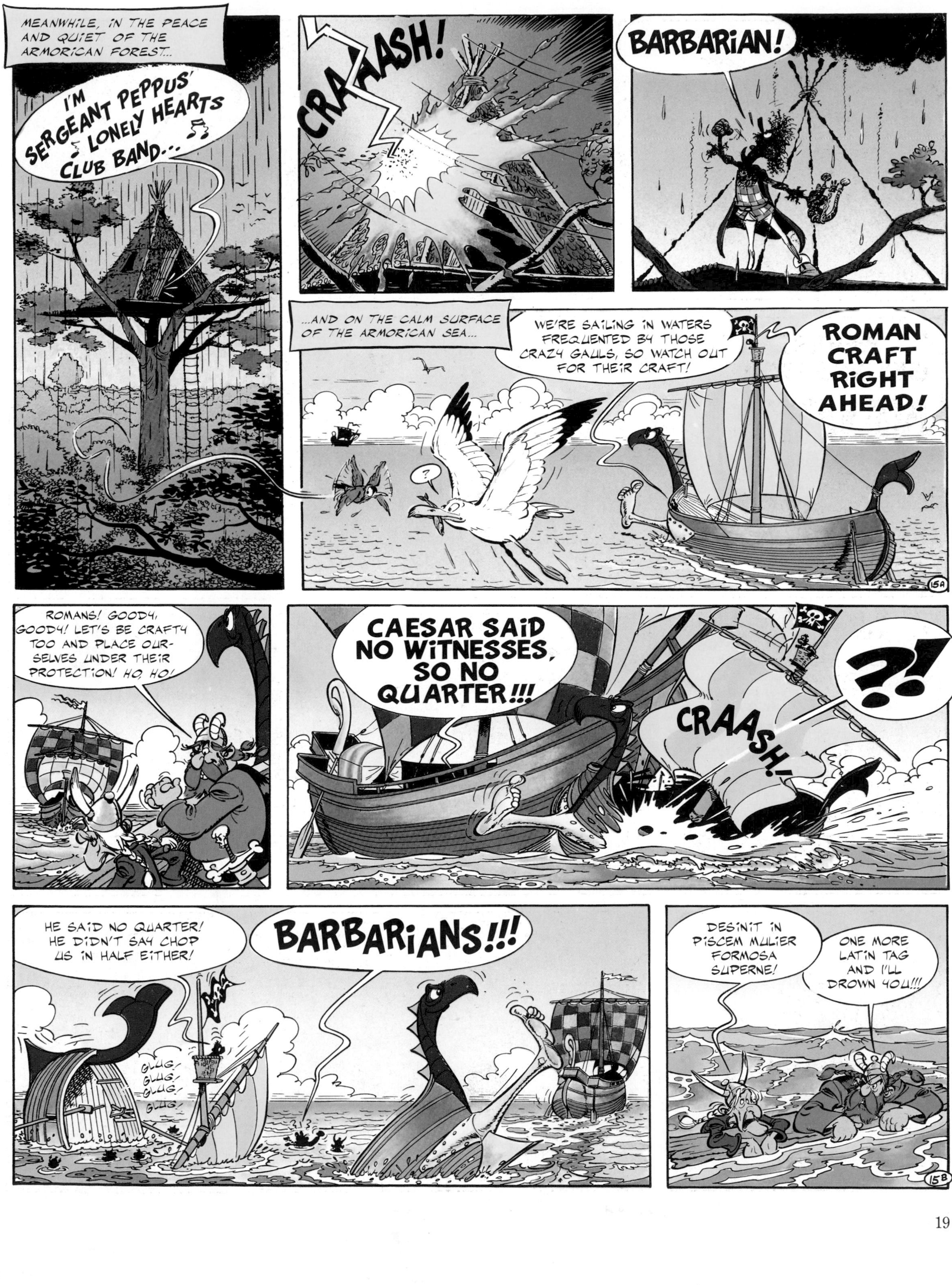
MEANWHILE, IN THE PEACE AND QUIET OF THE ARMORICAN FOREST...
I'M SERGEANT PEPPUS' LONELY HEARTS CLUB BAND...
CRAAASH!
BARBARIAN!
...AND ON THE CALM SURFACE OF THE ARMORICAN SEA...
WE'RE SAILING IN WATERS FREQUENTED BY THOSE CRAZY GAULS, SO WATCH OUT FOR THEIR CRAFT!
ROMAN CRAFT RIGHT AHEAD!
?
15A
ROMANS! GOODY, GOODY! LET'S BE CRAFTY TOO AND PLACE OURSELVES UNDER THEIR PROTECTION! HO, HO!
CAESAR SAID NO WITNESSES, SO NO QUARTER!!!
?!
CRAASH!
HE SAID NO QUARTER! HE DIDN'T SAY CHOP US IN HALF EITHER!
BARBARIANS!!!
GLUG! GLUG! GLUG! GLUG!
DESINIT IN PISCEM MULIER FORMOSA SUPERNE!
ONE MORE LATIN TAG AND I'LL DROWN YOU!!!
15B

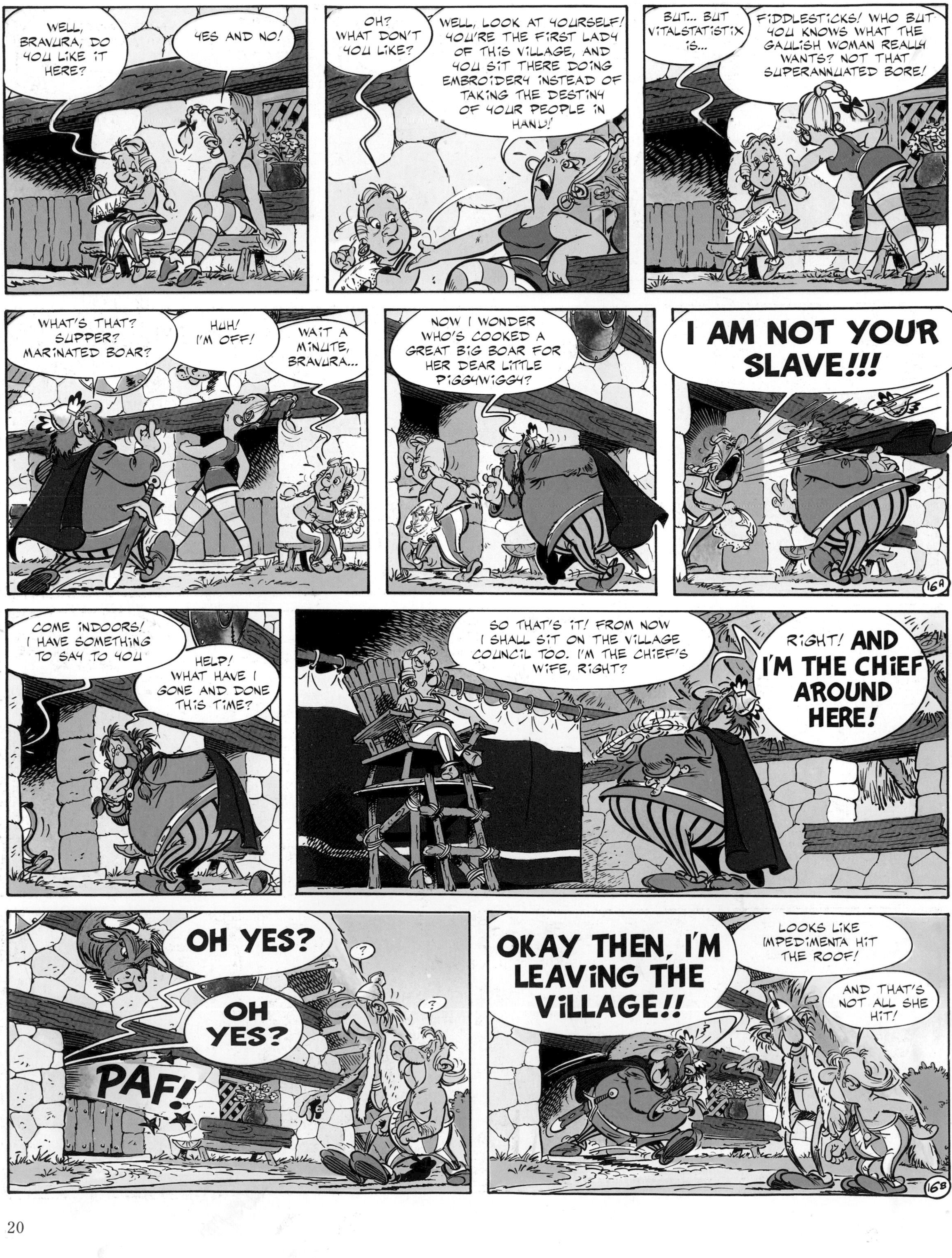
WELL, BRAVURA, DO YOU LIKE IT HERE?
YES AND NO!
OH? WHAT DON'T YOU LIKE?
WELL, LOOK AT YOURSELF! YOU'RE THE FIRST LADY OF THIS VILLAGE, AND YOU SIT THERE DOING EMBROIDERY INSTEAD OF TAKING THE DESTINY OF YOUR PEOPLE IN HAND!
BUT... BUT VITALSTATISTIX IS...
FIDDLESTICKS! WHO BUT YOU KNOWS WHAT THE GAULISH WOMAN REALLY WANTS? NOT THAT SUPERANNUATED BORE!
WHAT'S THAT? SUPPER? MARINATED BOAR?
HUH! I'M OFF!
WAIT A MINUTE, BRAVURA...
NOW I WONDER WHO'S COOKED A GREAT BIG BOAR FOR HER DEAR LITTLE PIGGYWIGGY?
I AM NOT YOUR SLAVE!!!
16A
COME INDOORS! I HAVE SOMETHING TO SAY TO YOU
HELP! WHAT HAVE I GONE AND DONE THIS TIME?
SO THAT'S IT! FROM NOW I SHALL SIT ON THE VILLAGE COUNCIL TOO. I'M THE CHIEF'S WIFE, RIGHT?
RIGHT! AND I'M THE CHIEF AROUND HERE!
OH YES?
?
OH YES?
?
PAF!
OKAY THEN, I'M LEAVING THE VILLAGE!!
LOOKS LIKE IMPEDIMENTA HIT THE ROOF!
AND THAT'S NOT ALL SHE HIT!
16B

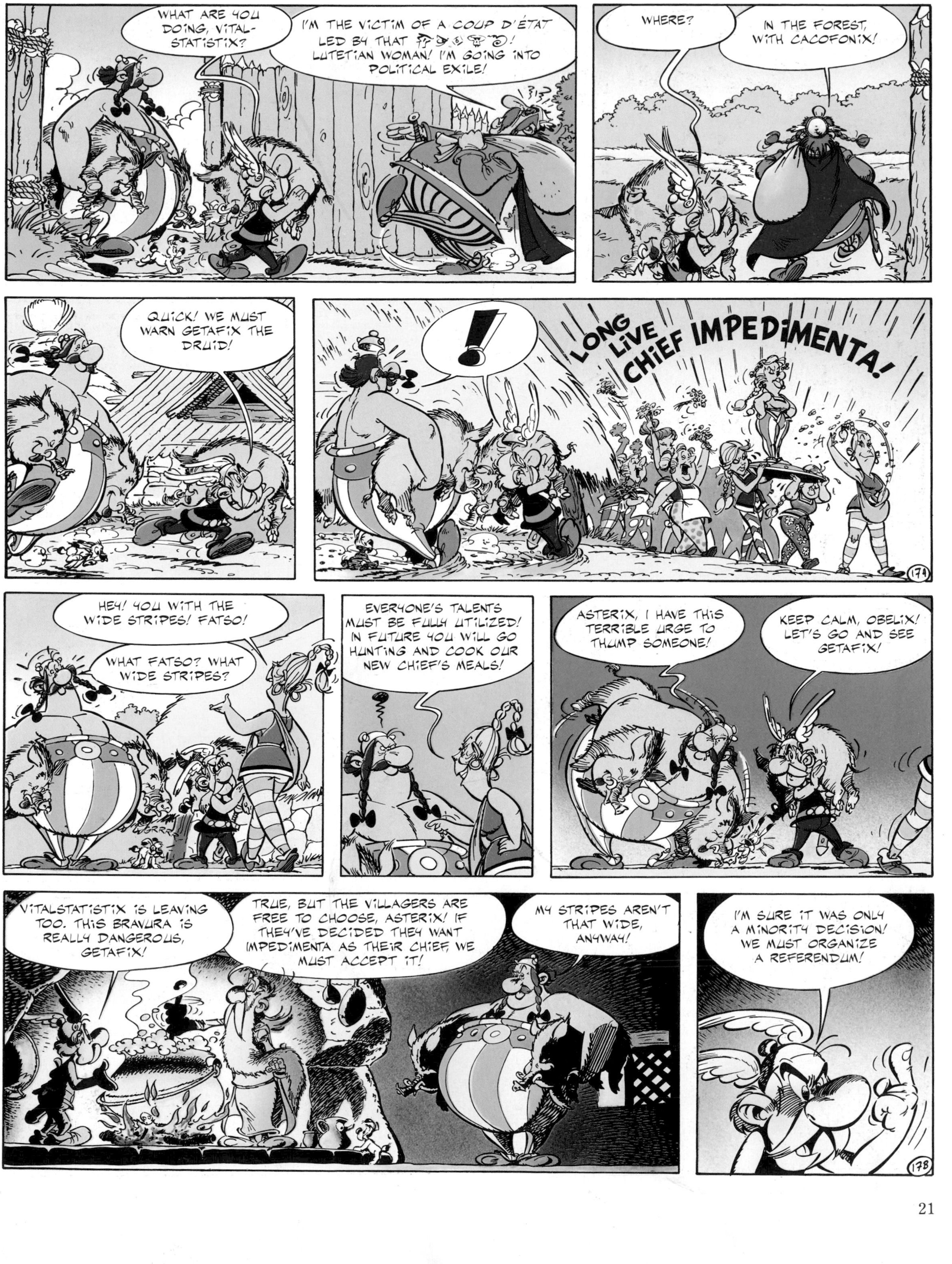
WHAT ARE YOU DOING, VITAL-STATISTIX?
I'M THE VICTIM OF A COUP D'ÉTAT LED BY THAT !! LUTETIAN WOMAN! I'M GOING INTO POLITICAL EXILE!
WHERE?
IN THE FOREST, WITH CACOFONIX!
QUICK! WE MUST WARN GETAFIX THE DRUID!
!
LONG LIVE CHIEF IMPEDIMENTA!
174
HEY! YOU WITH THE WIDE STRIPES! FATSO!
WHAT FATSO? WHAT WIDE STRIPES?
GRRR
EVERYONE'S TALENTS MUST BE FULLY UTILIZED! IN FUTURE YOU WILL GO HUNTING AND COOK OUR NEW CHIEF'S MEALS!
ASTERIX, I HAVE THIS TERRIBLE URGE TO THUMP SOMEONE!
KEEP CALM, OBELIX! LET'S GO AND SEE GETAFIX!
VITALSTATISTIX IS LEAVING TOO. THIS BRAVURA IS REALLY DANGEROUS, GETAFIX!
TRUE, BUT THE VILLAGERS ARE FREE TO CHOOSE, ASTERIX! IF THEY'VE DECIDED THEY WANT IMPEDIMENTA AS THEIR CHIEF, WE MUST ACCEPT IT!
MY STRIPES AREN'T THAT WIDE, ANYWAY!
I'M SURE IT WAS ONLY A MINORITY DECISION! WE MUST ORGANIZE A REFERENDUM!
178

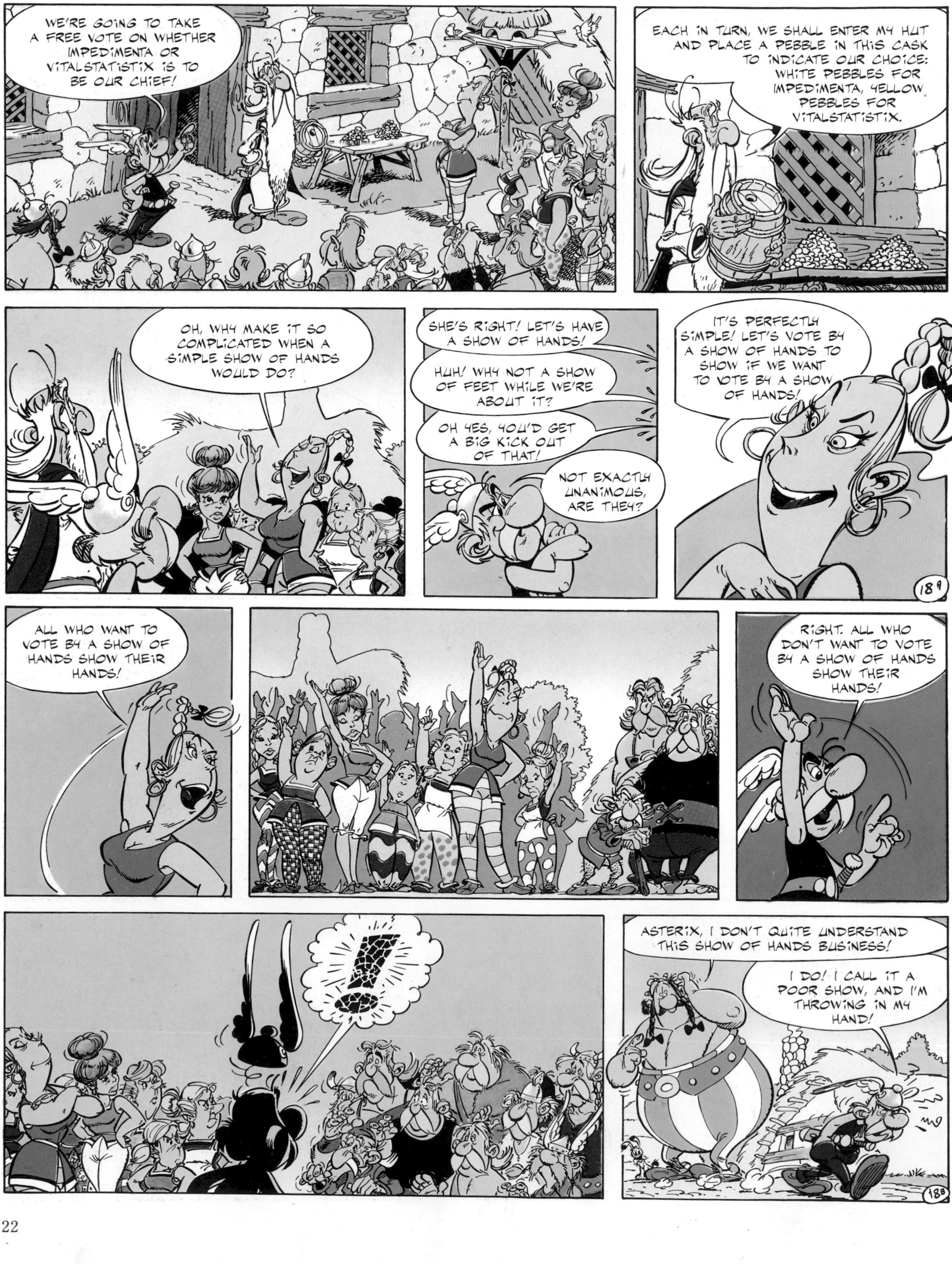
WE'RE GOING TO TAKE A FREE VOTE ON WHETHER IMPEDIMENTA OR VITALSTATISTIX IS TO BE OUR CHIEF!
EACH IN TURN, WE SHALL ENTER MY HUT AND PLACE A PEBBLE IN THIS CASK TO INDICATE OUR CHOICE: WHITE PEBBLES FOR IMPEDIMENTA, YELLOW PEBBLES FOR VITALSTATISTIX.
OH, WHY MAKE IT SO COMPLICATED WHEN A SIMPLE SHOW OF HANDS WOULD DO?
SHE'S RIGHT! LET'S HAVE A SHOW OF HANDS!
HUH! WHY NOT A SHOW OF FEET WHILE WE'RE ABOUT IT?
OH YES, YOU'D GET A BIG KICK OUT OF THAT!
NOT EXACTLY UNANIMOUS, ARE THEY?
IT'S PERFECTLY SIMPLE! LET'S VOTE BY A SHOW OF HANDS TO SHOW IF WE WANT TO VOTE BY A SHOW OF HANDS!
189
ALL WHO WANT TO VOTE BY A SHOW OF HANDS SHOW THEIR HANDS!
RIGHT. ALL WHO DON'T WANT TO VOTE BY A SHOW OF HANDS SHOW THEIR HANDS!
!
ASTERIX, I DON'T QUITE UNDERSTAND THIS SHOW OF HANDS BUSINESS!
I DO! I CALL IT A POOR SHOW, AND I'M THROWING IN MY HAND!
188

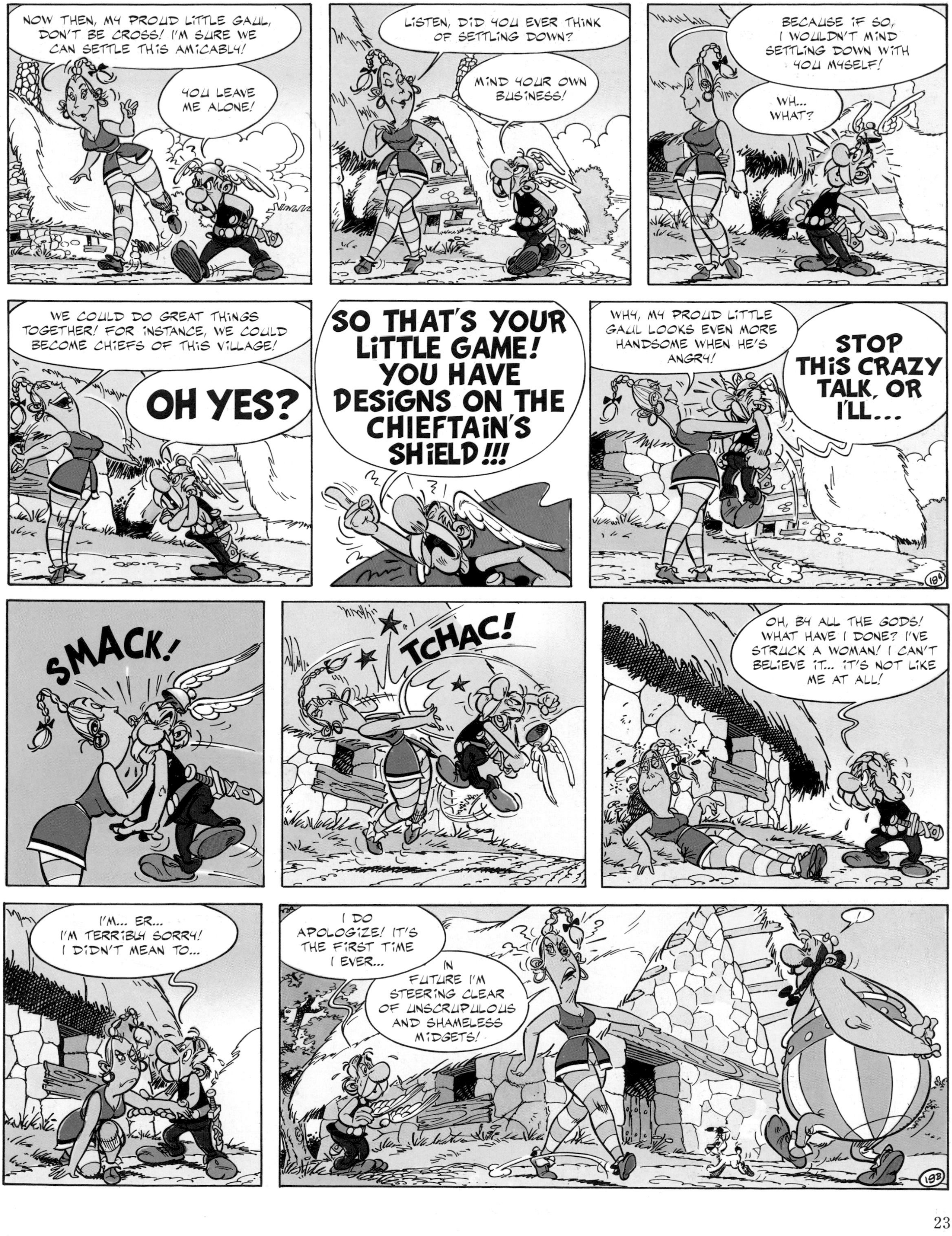
NOW THEN, MY PROUD LITTLE GAUL, DON'T BE CROSS! I'M SURE WE CAN SETTLE THIS AMICABLY!
YOU LEAVE ME ALONE!
LISTEN, DID YOU EVER THINK OF SETTLING DOWN?
MIND YOUR OWN BUSINESS!
BECAUSE IF SO, I WOULDN'T MIND SETTLING DOWN WITH YOU MYSELF!
WH... WHAT?
WE COULD DO GREAT THINGS TOGETHER! FOR INSTANCE, WE COULD BECOME CHIEFS OF THIS VILLAGE!
OH YES?
SO THAT'S YOUR LITTLE GAME! YOU HAVE DESIGNS ON THE CHIEFTAIN'S SHIELD!!!
WHY, MY PROUD LITTLE GAUL LOOKS EVEN MORE HANDSOME WHEN HE'S ANGRY!
STOP THIS CRAZY TALK, OR I'LL...
SMACK!
TCHAC!
OH, BY ALL THE GODS! WHAT HAVE I DONE? I'VE STRUCK A WOMAN! I CAN'T BELIEVE IT... IT'S NOT LIKE ME AT ALL!
I'M... ER... I'M TERRIBLY SORRY! I DIDN'T MEAN TO...
I DO APOLOGIZE! IT'S THE FIRST TIME I EVER...
IN FUTURE I'M STEERING CLEAR OF UNSCRUPULOUS AND SHAMELESS MIDGETS!
!

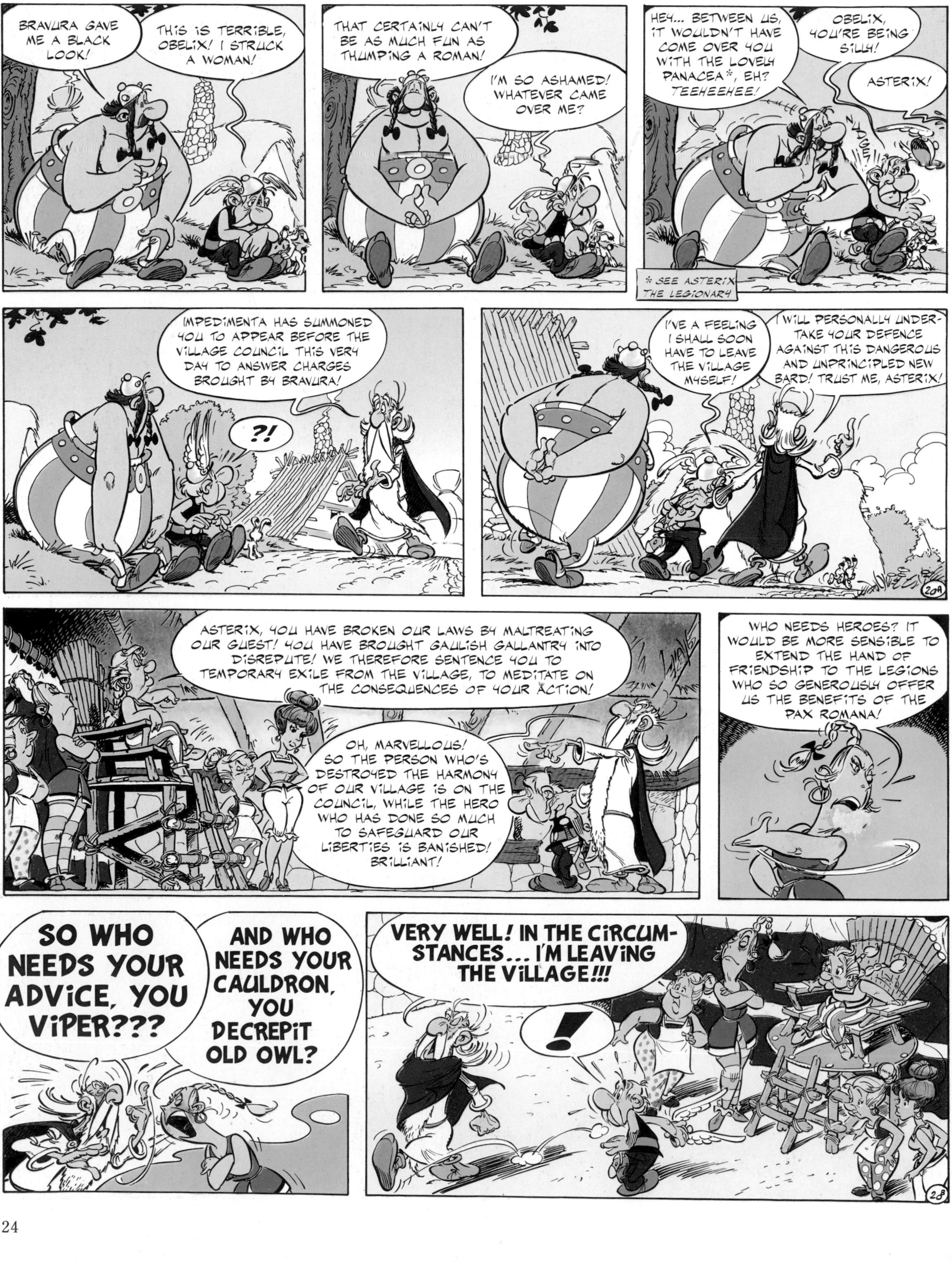
BRAVURA GAVE ME A BLACK LOOK!
THIS IS TERRIBLE, OBELIX! I STRUCK A WOMAN!
THAT CERTAINLY CAN'T BE AS MUCH FUN AS THUMPING A ROMAN!
I'M SO ASHAMED! WHATEVER CAME OVER ME?
HEY... BETWEEN US, IT WOULDN'T HAVE COME OVER YOU WITH THE LOVELY PANACEA*, EH? TEEHEEHEE!
OBELIX, YOU'RE BEING SILLY!
ASTERIX!
* SEE ASTERIX THE LEGIONARY
IMPEDIMENTA HAS SUMMONED YOU TO APPEAR BEFORE THE VILLAGE COUNCIL THIS VERY DAY TO ANSWER CHARGES BROUGHT BY BRAVURA!
?!
I'VE A FEELING I SHALL SOON HAVE TO LEAVE THE VILLAGE MYSELF!
I WILL PERSONALLY UNDERTAKE YOUR DEFENCE AGAINST THIS DANGEROUS AND UNPRINCIPLED NEW BARD! TRUST ME, ASTERIX!
ASTERIX, YOU HAVE BROKEN OUR LAWS BY MALTREATING OUR GUEST! YOU HAVE BROUGHT GAULISH GALLANTRY INTO DISREPUTE! WE THEREFORE SENTENCE YOU TO TEMPORARY EXILE FROM THE VILLAGE, TO MEDITATE ON THE CONSEQUENCES OF YOUR ACTION!
OH, MARVELLOUS! SO THE PERSON WHO'S DESTROYED THE HARMONY OF OUR VILLAGE IS ON THE COUNCIL, WHILE THE HERO WHO HAS DONE SO MUCH TO SAFEGUARD OUR LIBERTIES IS BANISHED! BRILLIANT!
WHO NEEDS HEROES? IT WOULD BE MORE SENSIBLE TO EXTEND THE HAND OF FRIENDSHIP TO THE LEGIONS WHO SO GENEROUSLY OFFER US THE BENEFITS OF THE PAX ROMANA!
SO WHO NEEDS YOUR ADVICE, YOU VIPER???
AND WHO NEEDS YOUR CAULDRON, YOU DECREPIT OLD OWL?
VERY WELL! IN THE CIRCUMSTANCES... I'M LEAVING THE VILLAGE!!!
!

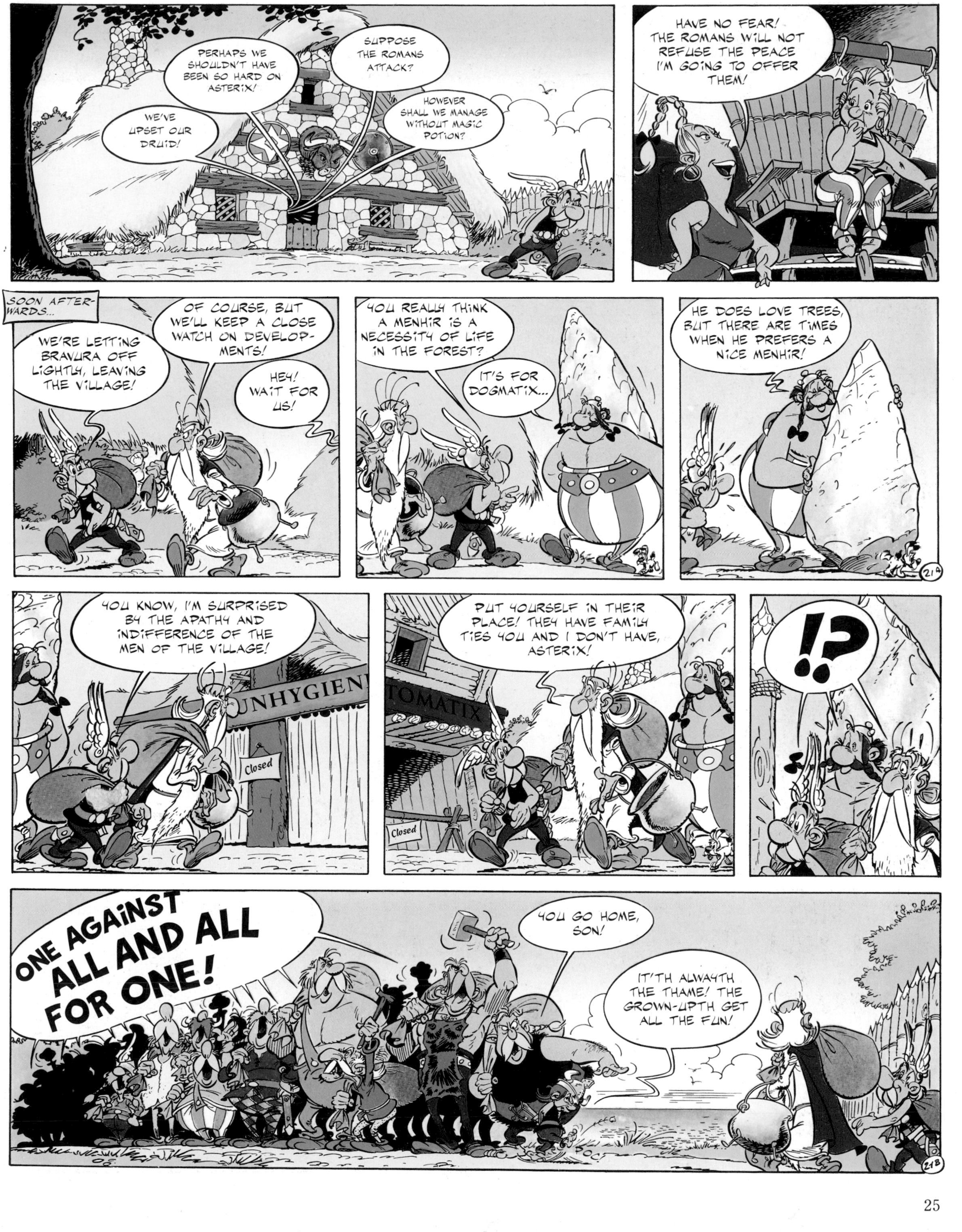
WE'VE UPSET OUR DRUID!
PERHAPS WE SHOULDN'T HAVE BEEN SO HARD ON ASTERIX!
SUPPOSE THE ROMANS ATTACK?
HOWEVER SHALL WE MANAGE WITHOUT MAGIC POTION?
HAVE NO FEAR! THE ROMANS WILL NOT REFUSE THE PEACE I'M GOING TO OFFER THEM!
SOON AFTERWARDS...
WE'RE LETTING BRAVURA OFF LIGHTLY, LEAVING THE VILLAGE!
OF COURSE, BUT WE'LL KEEP A CLOSE WATCH ON DEVELOPMENTS!
HEY! WAIT FOR US!
YOU REALLY THINK A MENHIR IS A NECESSITY OF LIFE IN THE FOREST?
IT'S FOR DOGMATIX...
HE DOES LOVE TREES, BUT THERE ARE TIMES WHEN HE PREFERS A NICE MENHIR!
YOU KNOW, I'M SURPRISED BY THE APATHY AND INDIFFERENCE OF THE MEN OF THE VILLAGE!
UNHYGIENI
Closed
PUT YOURSELF IN THEIR PLACE! THEY HAVE FAMILY TIES YOU AND I DON'T HAVE, ASTERIX!
TOMATIX
Closed
!?
ONE AGAINST ALL AND ALL FOR ONE!
YOU GO HOME, SON!
IT'TH ALWAYTH THE THAME! THE GROWN-UPTH GET ALL THE FUN!

MEANWHILE, ON THE COAST NEAR THE FORTIFIED CAMP OF AQUARIUM...
STAND BY TO DISEMBARK!
CREEEEAK!
OH FOR SOME NICE SEA AIR!
I'LL ASK YOU TO BE PATIENT A LITTLE LONGER. DON'T COME OUT BEFORE I GIVE THE ORDER!
AND IN THE FORTIFIED CAMP OF AQUARIUM...
SNIFF! THE GAULS HAB GOT A FORBID-ABLE ABD DABGEROUS WEAPOB...
...THEIR WRETCHEB BARB WHO CAB OBLY SING SO BADLY...
...THAT HE BRINGS DOWB THE CURSE OF THE GOBS WHEBEVER HE SINGS!
?!
BLOW!
QUOB ERAT BEMONSTRANBAAA...
TISHOOO!
IT'LL BE A GREAT RELIEF WHEN THE RELIEF GETS HERE!
THE RELIEF'S HERE, CENTURION!
229
ARE... ARE YOU THE RELIEF?
SO TO SPEAK! MY ORDERS FROM CAESAR ARE TO TELL YOU TO LEAVE CAMP BEFORE THE RELIEF RELIEVES YOU!
AND SUPPOSE I REFUSE TO LEAVE CAMP BEFORE THE RELIEF RELIEVES US?
THEN YOU'LL BE RELIEVED OF YOUR DUTIES AND GO TO RELIEVE THE MONOTONY OF THE DIET OF THE LIONS IN THE CIRCUS!
WE'RE LEAVING CAMP!
MEANWHILE, IN THE FOREST SEPARATING THE VILLAGE FROM THE ROMAN CAMP...
WE'RE NOT TOO BADLY OFF HERE WHILE WE WAIT FOR OUR GOOD LADIES TO SEE SENSE!
BUT WE MUST BE ON OUR GUARD, IN CASE THE ROMANS TAKE THEIR CHANCE TO SEIZE THE VILLAGE!
OBELIX AND I WILL GO AND KEEP WATCH ON THEM!
228

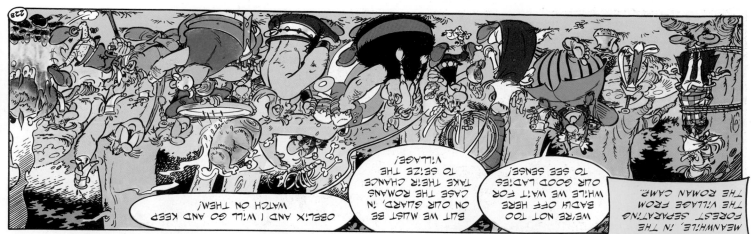

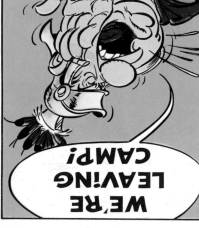

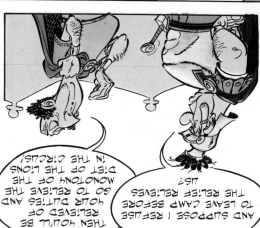

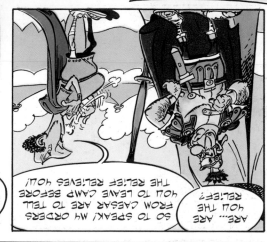

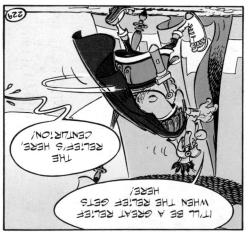

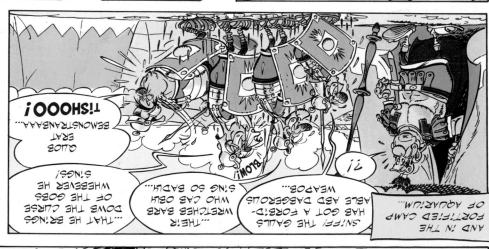

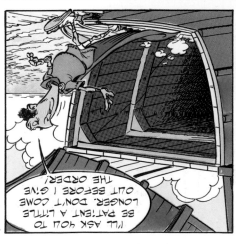

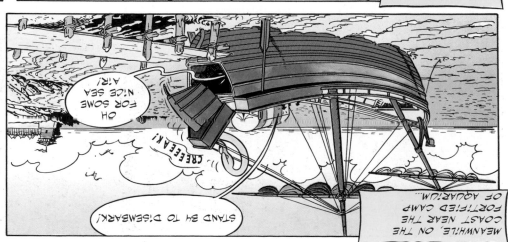

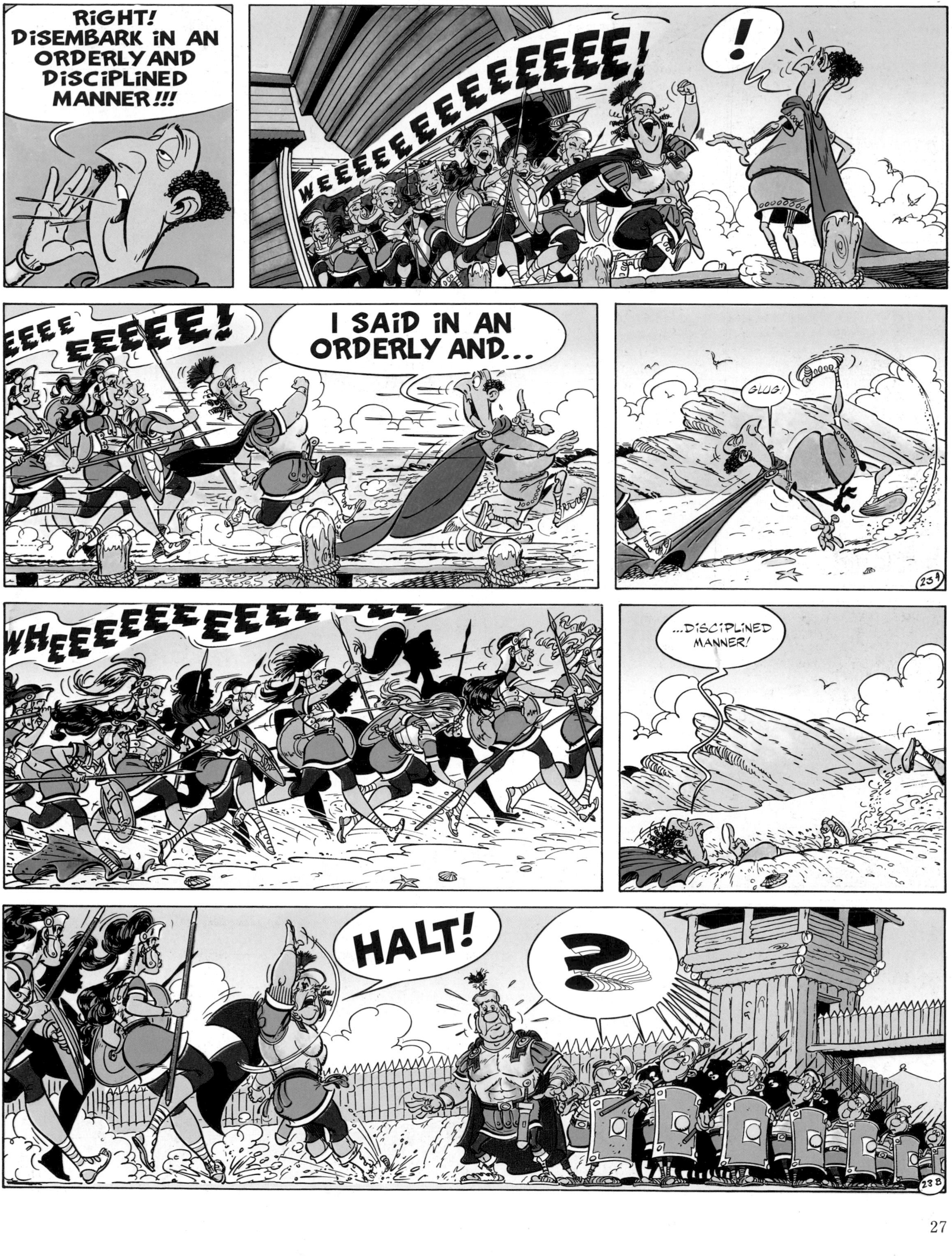
RIGHT! DISEMBARK IN AN ORDERLY AND DISCIPLINED MANNER!!!
WEEEEEEEEEEEEEEEEE!
!
EEEE EEEEE!
I SAID IN AN ORDERLY AND...
GLUG!
WHEEEEEEEEEEEEEE
...DISCIPLINED MANNER!
HALT!
?

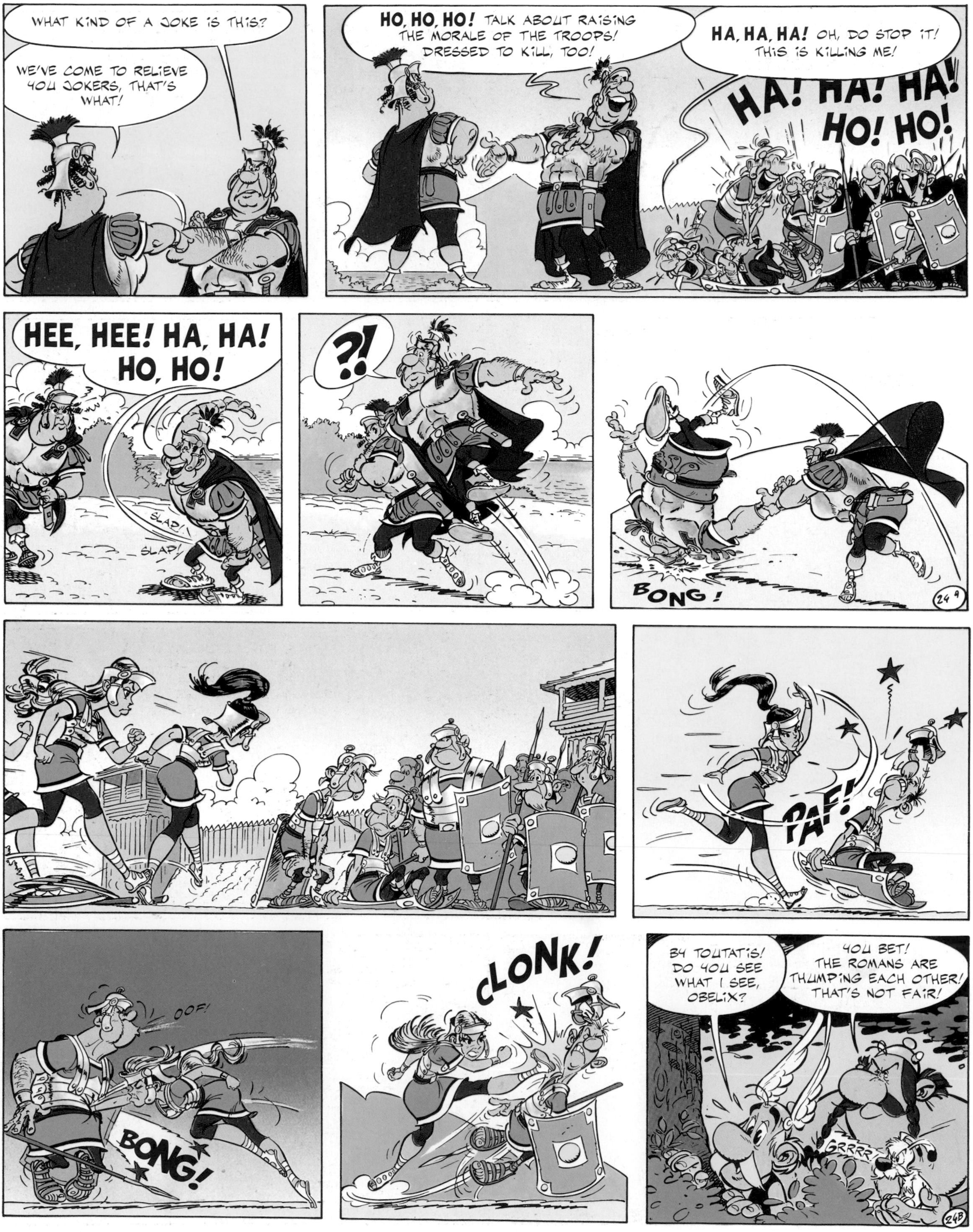

WHAT KIND OF A JOKE IS THIS?
WE'VE COME TO RELIEVE YOU JOKERS, THAT'S WHAT!
HO, HO, HO! TALK ABOUT RAISING THE MORALE OF THE TROOPS! DRESSED TO KILL, TOO!
HA, HA, HA! OH, DO STOP IT! THIS IS KILLING ME!
HA! HA! HA! HO! HO!
HEE, HEE! HA, HA! HO, HO!
SLAP!
SLAP!
?!
BONG!
PAF!
OOF!
BONG!
CLONK!
BY TOUTATIS! DO YOU SEE WHAT I SEE, OBELIX?
YOU BET! THE ROMANS ARE THUMPING EACH OTHER! THAT'S NOT FAIR!
GRRRR

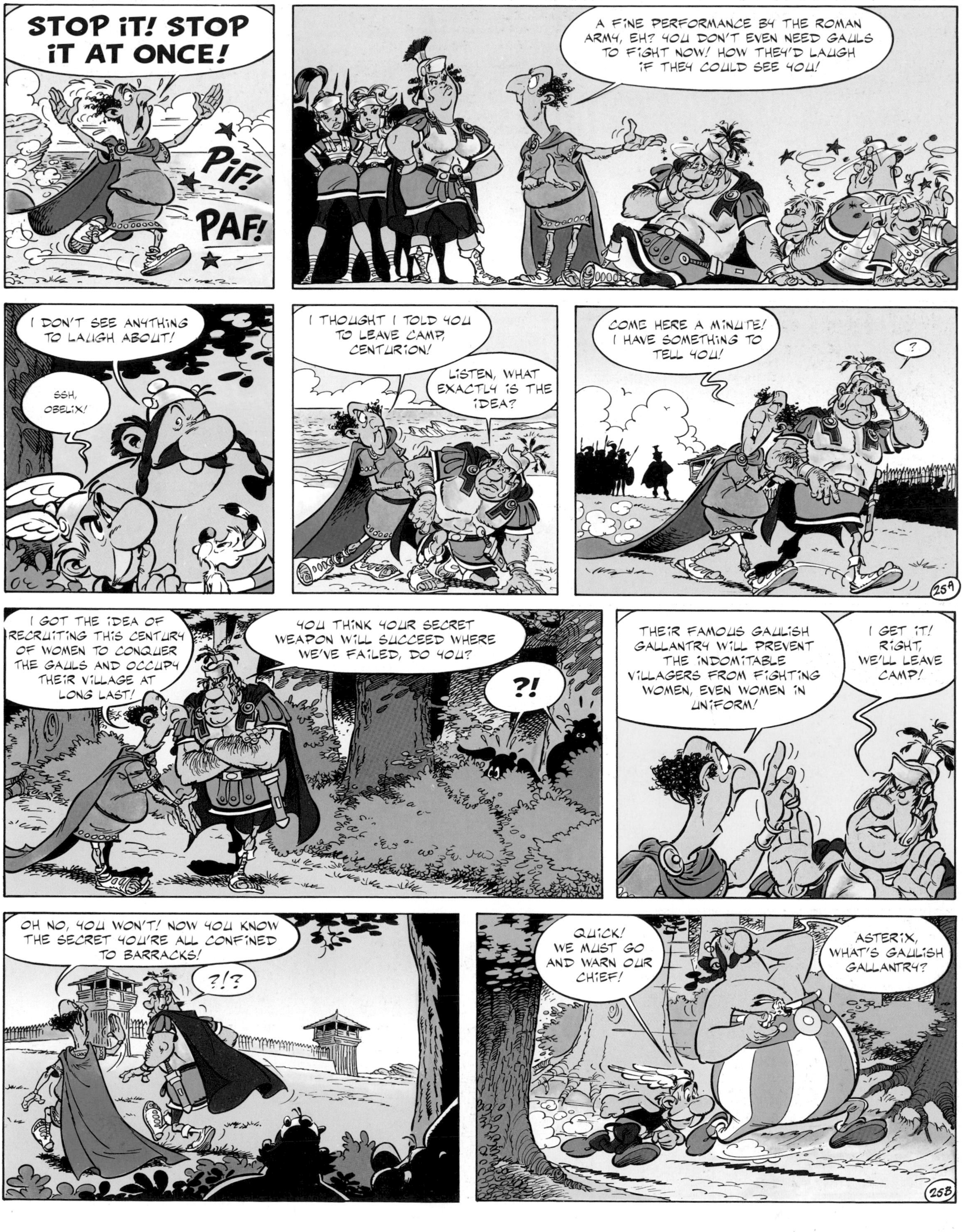
STOP iT! STOP iT AT ONCE!
PiF!
PAF!
A FiNE PERFORMANCE BY THE ROMAN ARMY, EH? YOU DON'T EVEN NEED GAULS TO FiGHT NOW! HOW THEY'D LAUGH iF THEY COULD SEE YOU!
I DON'T SEE ANYTHiNG TO LAUGH ABOUT!
SSH, OBELiX!
I THOUGHT I TOLD YOU TO LEAVE CAMP, CENTURiON!
LiSTEN, WHAT EXACTLY iS THE iDEA?
COME HERE A MiNUTE! I HAVE SOMETHiNG TO TELL YOU!
?
259
I GOT THE iDEA OF RECRUiTiNG THiS CENTURY OF WOMEN TO CONQUER THE GAULS AND OCCUPY THEiR ViLLAGE AT LONG LAST!
YOU THiNK YOUR SECRET WEAPON WiLL SUCCEED WHERE WE'VE FAiLED, DO YOU?
?!
THEiR FAMOUS GAULiSH GALLANTRY WiLL PREVENT THE iNDOMiTABLE ViLLAGERS FROM FiGHTiNG WOMEN, EVEN WOMEN iN UNiFORM!
I GET iT! RiGHT, WE'LL LEAVE CAMP!
OH NO, YOU WON'T! NOW YOU KNOW THE SECRET YOU'RE ALL CONFiNED TO BARRACKS!
?!?
QUiCK! WE MUST GO AND WARN OUR CHiEF!
ASTERiX, WHAT'S GAULiSH GALLANTRY?
258

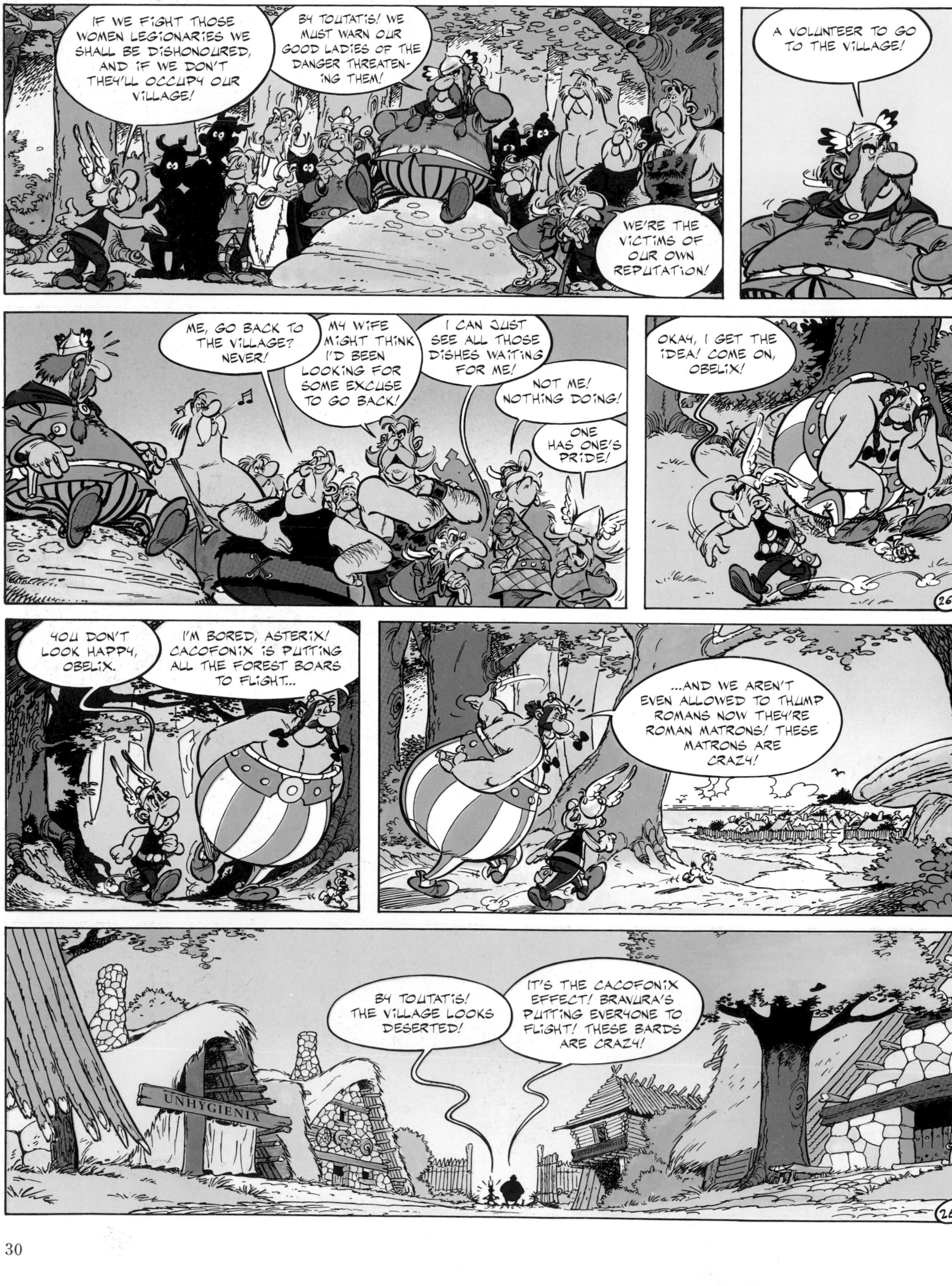
IF WE FIGHT THOSE WOMEN LEGIONARIES WE SHALL BE DISHONOURED, AND IF WE DON'T THEY'LL OCCUPY OUR VILLAGE!
BY TOUTATIS! WE MUST WARN OUR GOOD LADIES OF THE DANGER THREATENING THEM!
WE'RE THE VICTIMS OF OUR OWN REPUTATION!
A VOLUNTEER TO GO TO THE VILLAGE!
ME, GO BACK TO THE VILLAGE? NEVER!
MY WIFE MIGHT THINK I'D BEEN LOOKING FOR SOME EXCUSE TO GO BACK!
I CAN JUST SEE ALL THOSE DISHES WAITING FOR ME!
NOT ME! NOTHING DOING!
ONE HAS ONE'S PRIDE!
OKAY, I GET THE IDEA! COME ON, OBELIX!
26A
YOU DON'T LOOK HAPPY, OBELIX.
I'M BORED, ASTERIX! CACOFONIX IS PUTTING ALL THE FOREST BOARS TO FLIGHT...
...AND WE AREN'T EVEN ALLOWED TO THUMP ROMANS NOW THEY'RE ROMAN MATRONS! THESE MATRONS ARE CRAZY!
UNHYGIENIX
BY TOUTATIS! THE VILLAGE LOOKS DESERTED!
IT'S THE CACOFONIX EFFECT! BRAVURA'S PUTTING EVERYONE TO FLIGHT! THESE BARDS ARE CRAZY!
26B

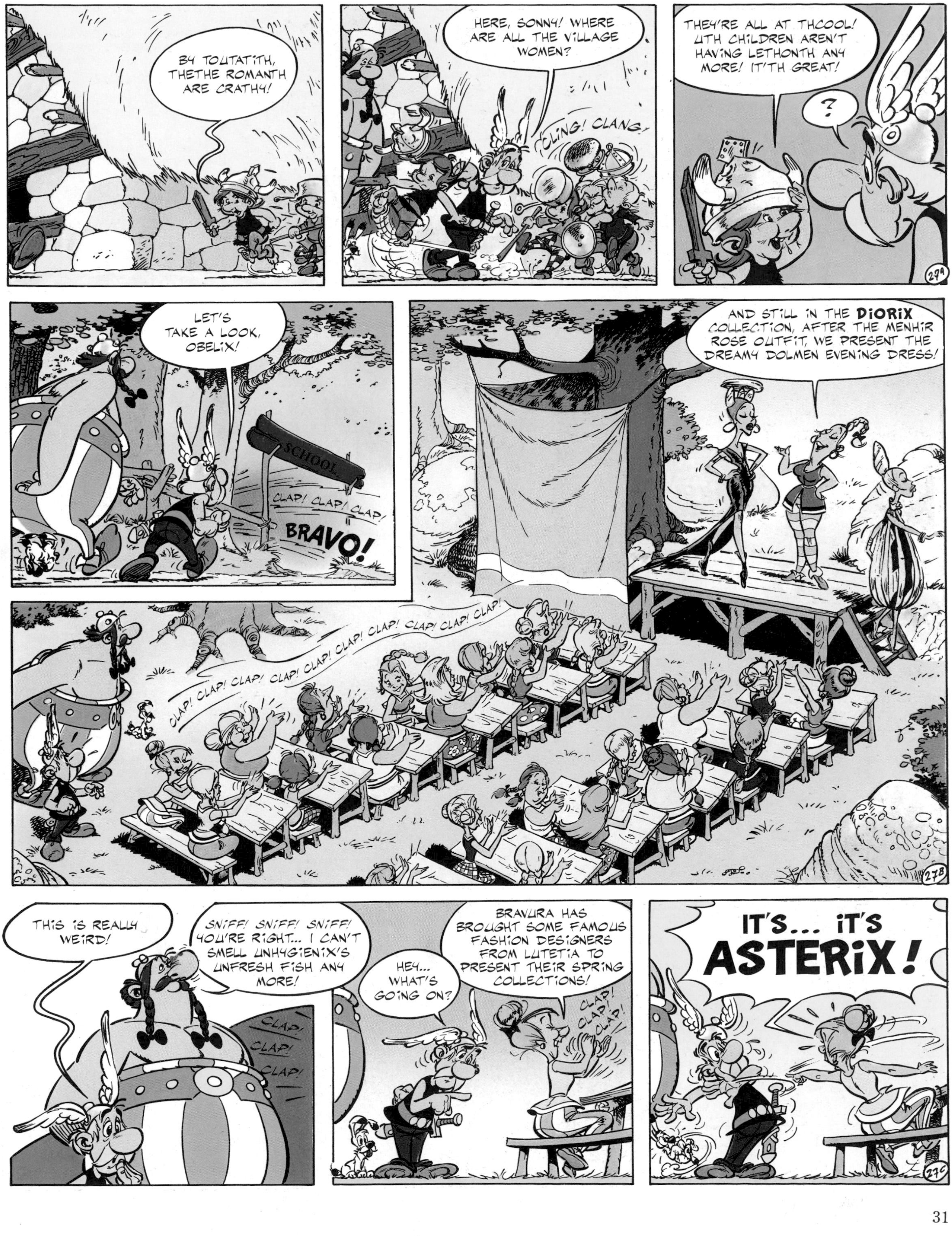
BY TOUTATITH, THETHE ROMANTH ARE CRATHY!
HERE, SONNY! WHERE ARE ALL THE VILLAGE WOMEN?
CLING! CLANG!
THEY'RE ALL AT THCOOL! UTH CHILDREN AREN'T HAVING LETHONTH ANY MORE! IT'TH GREAT!
?
LET'S TAKE A LOOK, OBELIX!
SCHOOL
CLAP! CLAP! CLAP!
BRAVO!
AND STILL IN THE DIORIX COLLECTION, AFTER THE MENHIR ROSE OUTFIT, WE PRESENT THE DREAMY DOLMEN EVENING DRESS!
CLAP! CLAP! CLAP! CLAP! CLAP! CLAP! CLAP! CLAP! CLAP! CLAP! CLAP!
THIS IS REALLY WEIRD!
SNIFF! SNIFF! SNIFF! YOU'RE RIGHT... I CAN'T SMELL UNHYGIENIX'S UNFRESH FISH ANY MORE!
CLAP! CLAP! CLAP!
HEY... WHAT'S GOING ON?
BRAVURA HAS BROUGHT SOME FAMOUS FASHION DESIGNERS FROM LUTETIA TO PRESENT THEIR SPRING COLLECTIONS!
CLAP! CLAP! CLAP!
IT'S... IT'S ASTERIX!

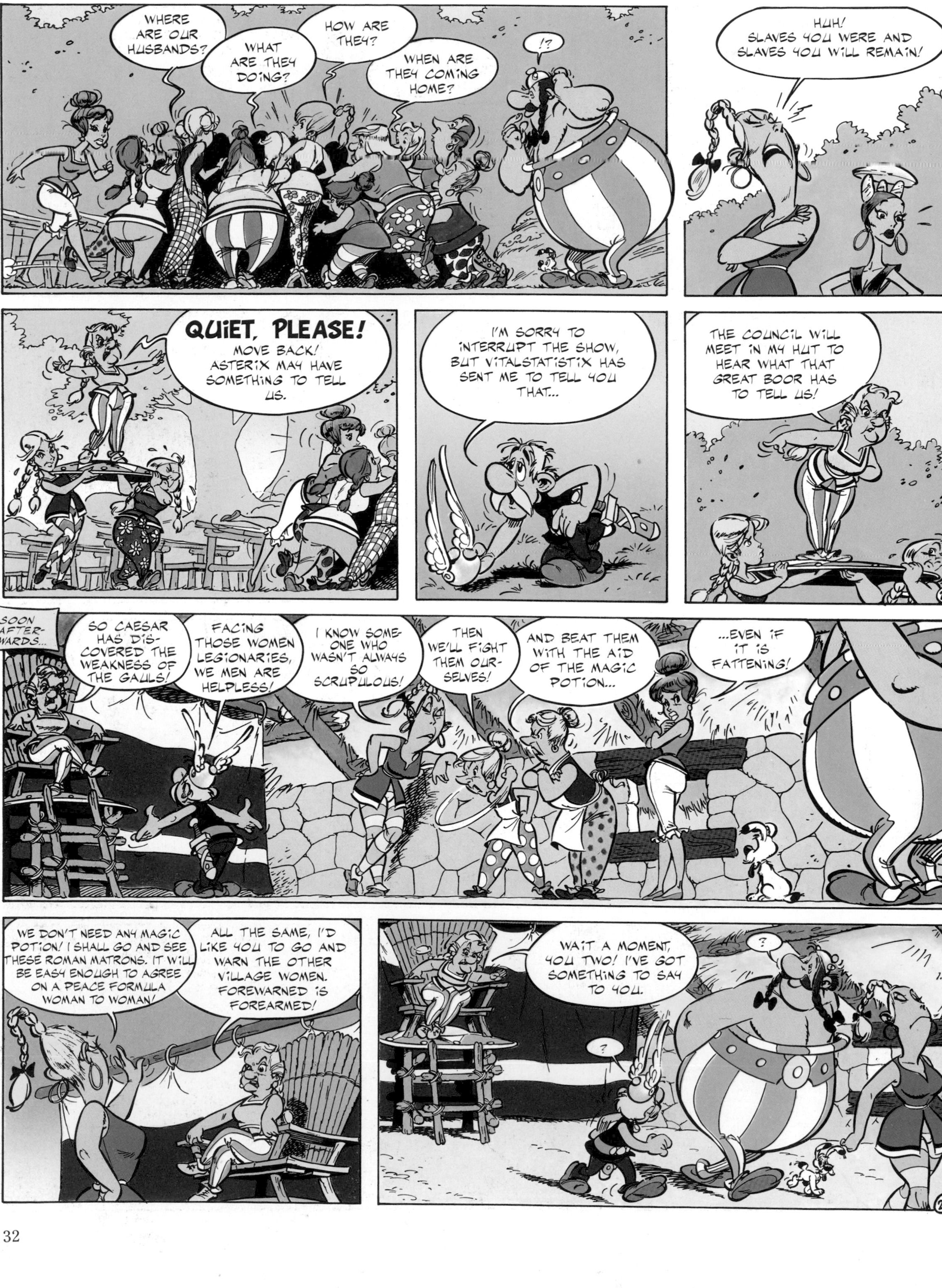

WHERE ARE OUR HUSBANDS?
WHAT ARE THEY DOING?
HOW ARE THEY?
WHEN ARE THEY COMING HOME?
!?
HUH! SLAVES YOU WERE AND SLAVES YOU WILL REMAIN!
QUIET, PLEASE! MOVE BACK! ASTERIX MAY HAVE SOMETHING TO TELL US.
I'M SORRY TO INTERRUPT THE SHOW, BUT VITALSTATISTIX HAS SENT ME TO TELL YOU THAT...
THE COUNCIL WILL MEET IN MY HUT TO HEAR WHAT THAT GREAT BOOR HAS TO TELL US!
SOON AFTERWARDS...
SO CAESAR HAS DISCOVERED THE WEAKNESS OF THE GAULS!
FACING THOSE WOMEN LEGIONARIES, WE MEN ARE HELPLESS!
I KNOW SOMEONE WHO WASN'T ALWAYS SO SCRUPULOUS!
THEN WE'LL FIGHT THEM OURSELVES!
AND BEAT THEM WITH THE AID OF THE MAGIC POTION...
...EVEN IF IT IS FATTENING!
WE DON'T NEED ANY MAGIC POTION! I SHALL GO AND SEE THESE ROMAN MATRONS. IT WILL BE EASY ENOUGH TO AGREE ON A PEACE FORMULA WOMAN TO WOMAN!
ALL THE SAME, I'D LIKE YOU TO GO AND WARN THE OTHER VILLAGE WOMEN. FOREWARNED IS FOREARMED!
WAIT A MOMENT, YOU TWO! I'VE GOT SOMETHING TO SAY TO YOU.
?
?

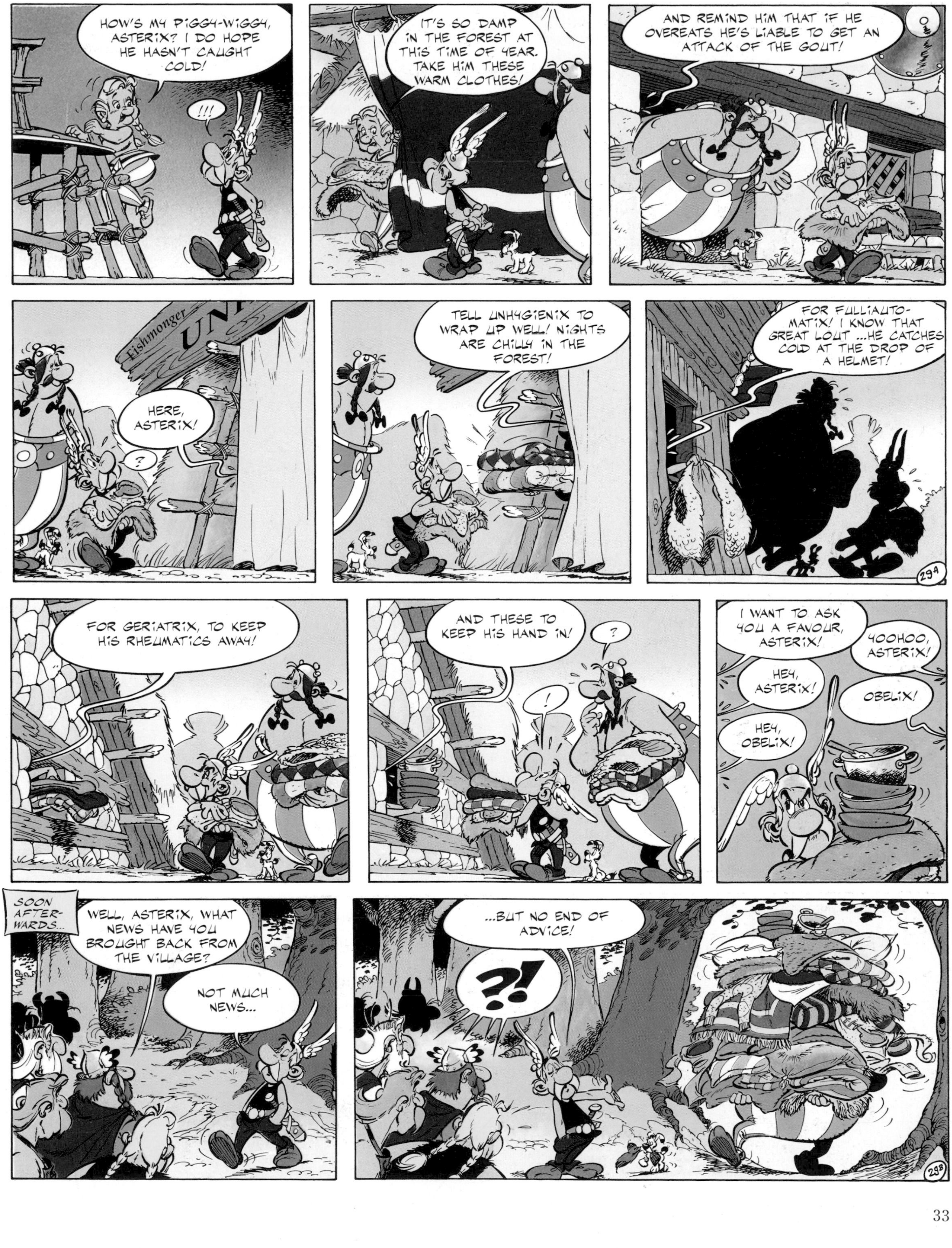
HOW'S MY PIGGY-WIGGY, ASTERIX? I DO HOPE HE HASN'T CAUGHT COLD!
!!!
IT'S SO DAMP IN THE FOREST AT THIS TIME OF YEAR. TAKE HIM THESE WARM CLOTHES!
AND REMIND HIM THAT IF HE OVEREATS HE'S LIABLE TO GET AN ATTACK OF THE GOUT!
Fishmonger
HERE, ASTERIX!
?
TELL UNHYGIENIX TO WRAP UP WELL! NIGHTS ARE CHILLY IN THE FOREST!
FOR FULLIAUTOMATIX! I KNOW THAT GREAT LOUT ...HE CATCHES COLD AT THE DROP OF A HELMET!
29A
FOR GERIATRIX, TO KEEP HIS RHEUMATICS AWAY!
AND THESE TO KEEP HIS HAND IN!
?
!
I WANT TO ASK YOU A FAVOUR, ASTERIX!
YOOHOO, ASTERIX!
HEY, ASTERIX!
OBELIX!
HEY, OBELIX!
SOON AFTERWARDS...
WELL, ASTERIX, WHAT NEWS HAVE YOU BROUGHT BACK FROM THE VILLAGE?
NOT MUCH NEWS...
...BUT NO END OF ADVICE!
?!
29B

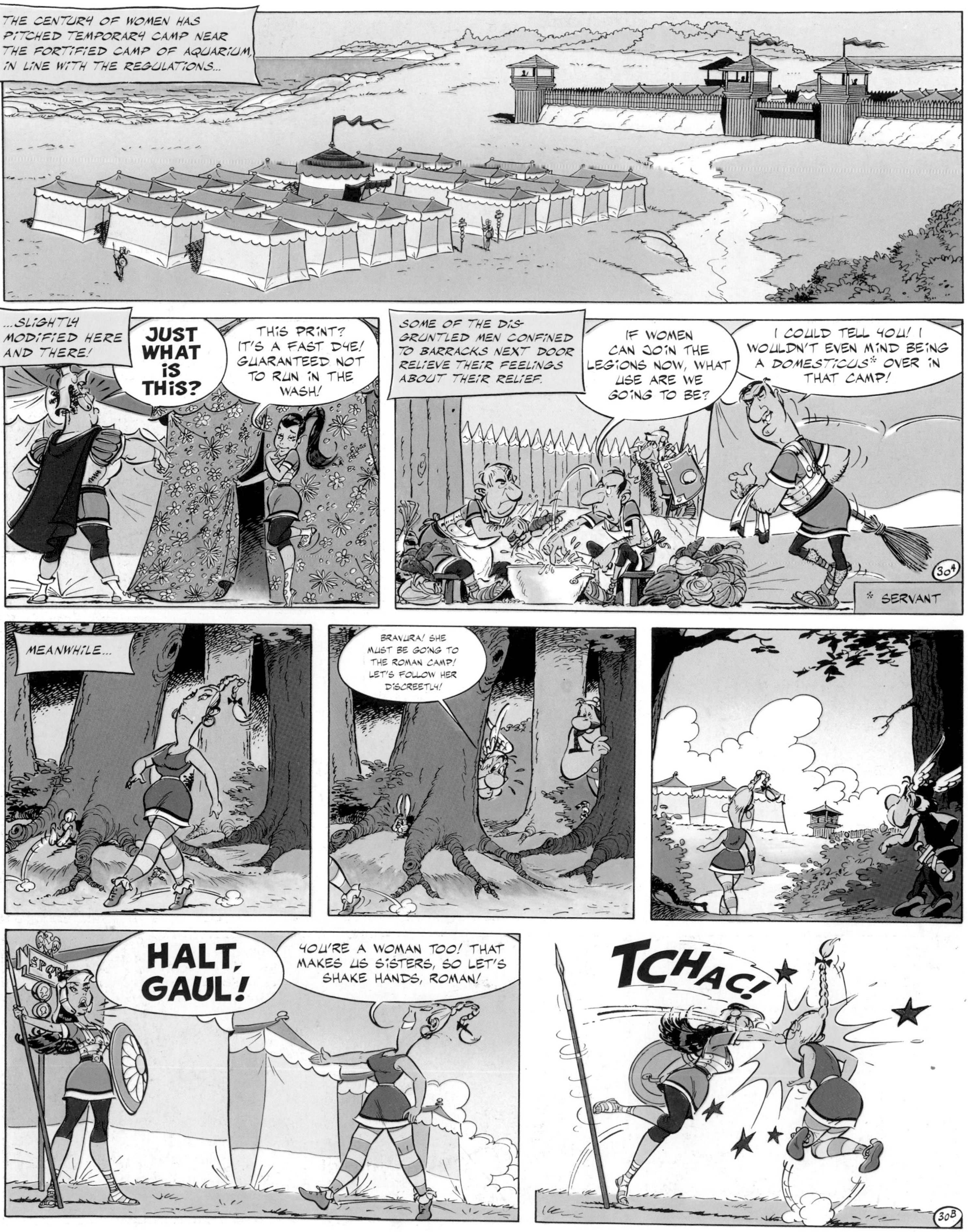
THE CENTURY OF WOMEN HAS PITCHED TEMPORARY CAMP NEAR THE FORTIFIED CAMP OF AQUARIUM, IN LINE WITH THE REGULATIONS...
...SLIGHTLY MODIFIED HERE AND THERE!
JUST WHAT IS THIS?
THIS PRINT? IT'S A FAST DYE! GUARANTEED NOT TO RUN IN THE WASH!
SOME OF THE DISGRUNTLED MEN CONFINED TO BARRACKS NEXT DOOR RELIEVE THEIR FEELINGS ABOUT THEIR RELIEF.
IF WOMEN CAN JOIN THE LEGIONS NOW, WHAT USE ARE WE GOING TO BE?
I COULD TELL YOU! I WOULDN'T EVEN MIND BEING A DOMESTICUS* OVER IN THAT CAMP!
30A
* SERVANT
MEANWHILE...
BRAVURA! SHE MUST BE GOING TO THE ROMAN CAMP! LET'S FOLLOW HER DISCREETLY!
HALT, GAUL!
SPQR
YOU'RE A WOMAN TOO! THAT MAKES US SISTERS, SO LET'S SHAKE HANDS, ROMAN!
TCHAC!
30B

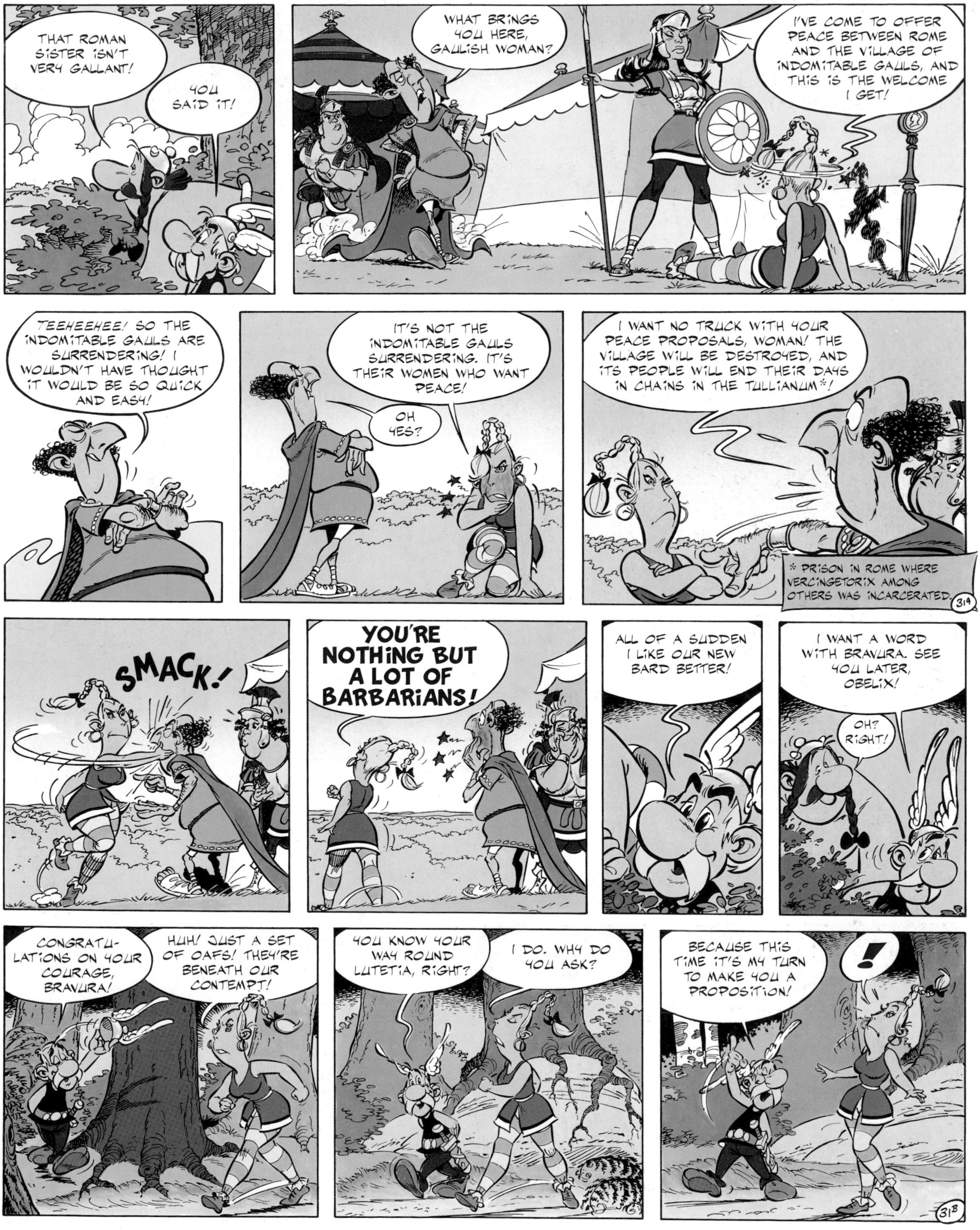
THAT ROMAN SISTER ISN'T VERY GALLANT!
YOU SAID IT!
WHAT BRINGS YOU HERE, GAULISH WOMAN?
I'VE COME TO OFFER PEACE BETWEEN ROME AND THE VILLAGE OF INDOMITABLE GAULS, AND THIS IS THE WELCOME I GET!
TEEHEEHEE! SO THE INDOMITABLE GAULS ARE SURRENDERING! I WOULDN'T HAVE THOUGHT IT WOULD BE SO QUICK AND EASY!
IT'S NOT THE INDOMITABLE GAULS SURRENDERING. IT'S THEIR WOMEN WHO WANT PEACE!
OH YES?
I WANT NO TRUCK WITH YOUR PEACE PROPOSALS, WOMAN! THE VILLAGE WILL BE DESTROYED, AND ITS PEOPLE WILL END THEIR DAYS IN CHAINS IN THE TULLIANUM*!
* PRISON IN ROME WHERE VERCINGETORIX AMONG OTHERS WAS INCARCERATED.
SMACK!
YOU'RE NOTHING BUT A LOT OF BARBARIANS!
ALL OF A SUDDEN I LIKE OUR NEW BARD BETTER!
I WANT A WORD WITH BRAVURA. SEE YOU LATER, OBELIX!
OH? RIGHT!
CONGRATU-LATIONS ON YOUR COURAGE, BRAVURA!
HUH! JUST A SET OF OAFS! THEY'RE BENEATH OUR CONTEMPT!
YOU KNOW YOUR WAY ROUND LUTETIA, RIGHT?
I DO. WHY DO YOU ASK?
BECAUSE THIS TIME IT'S MY TURN TO MAKE YOU A PROPOSITION!
!

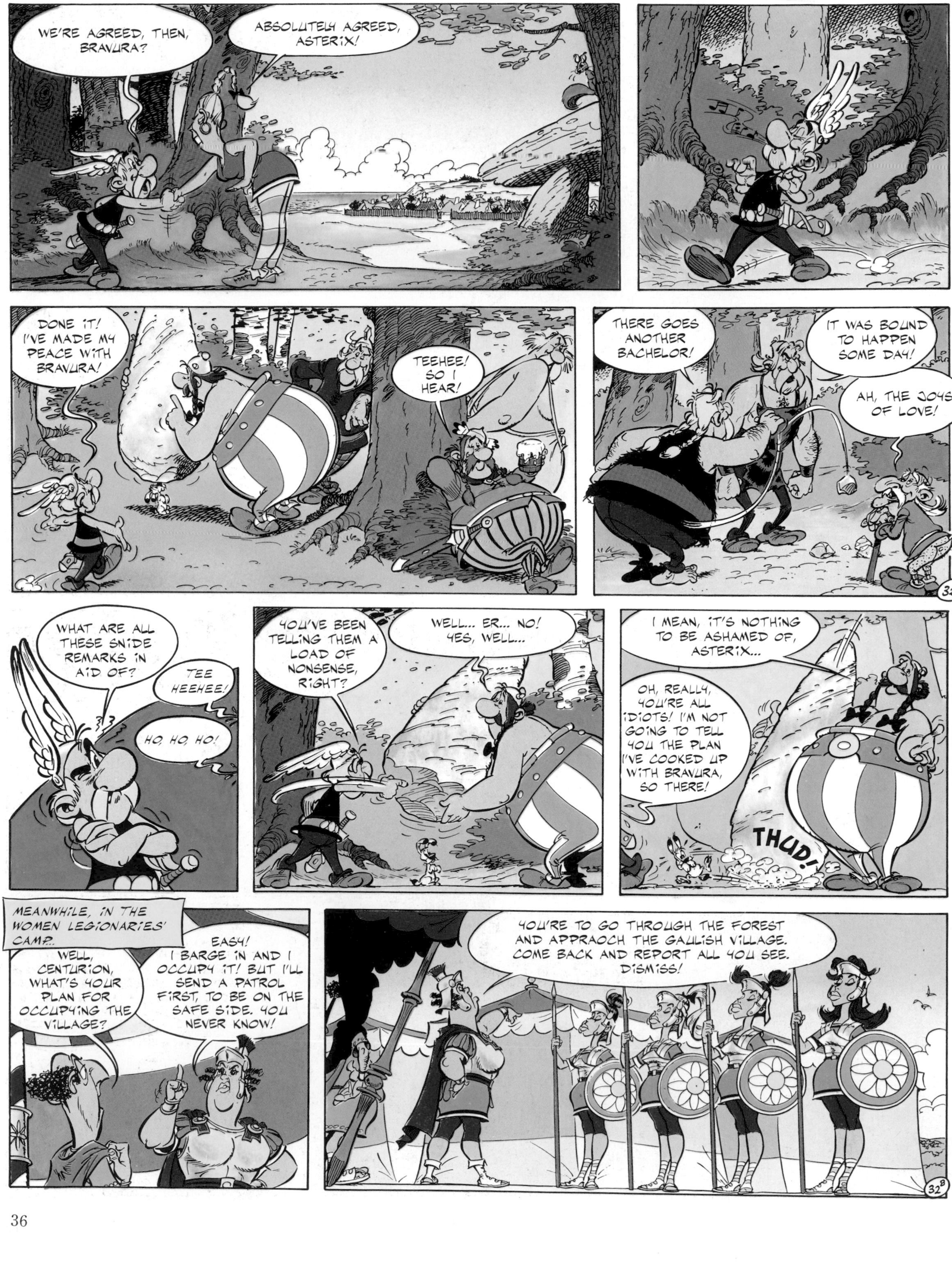
WE'RE AGREED, THEN, BRAVURA?
ABSOLUTELY AGREED, ASTERIX!
DONE IT! I'VE MADE MY PEACE WITH BRAVURA!
TEEHEE! SO I HEAR!
THERE GOES ANOTHER BACHELOR!
IT WAS BOUND TO HAPPEN SOME DAY!
AH, THE JOYS OF LOVE!
WHAT ARE ALL THESE SNIDE REMARKS IN AID OF?
TEE HEEHEE!
HO, HO, HO!
YOU'VE BEEN TELLING THEM A LOAD OF NONSENSE, RIGHT?
WELL... ER... NO! YES, WELL...
I MEAN, IT'S NOTHING TO BE ASHAMED OF, ASTERIX...
OH, REALLY, YOU'RE ALL IDIOTS! I'M NOT GOING TO TELL YOU THE PLAN I'VE COOKED UP WITH BRAVURA, SO THERE!
THUD!
MEANWHILE, IN THE WOMEN LEGIONARIES' CAMP...
WELL, CENTURION, WHAT'S YOUR PLAN FOR OCCUPYING THE VILLAGE?
EASY! I BARGE IN AND I OCCUPY IT! BUT I'LL SEND A PATROL FIRST, TO BE ON THE SAFE SIDE. YOU NEVER KNOW!
YOU'RE TO GO THROUGH THE FOREST AND APPRAOCH THE GAULISH VILLAGE. COME BACK AND REPORT ALL YOU SEE. DISMISS!

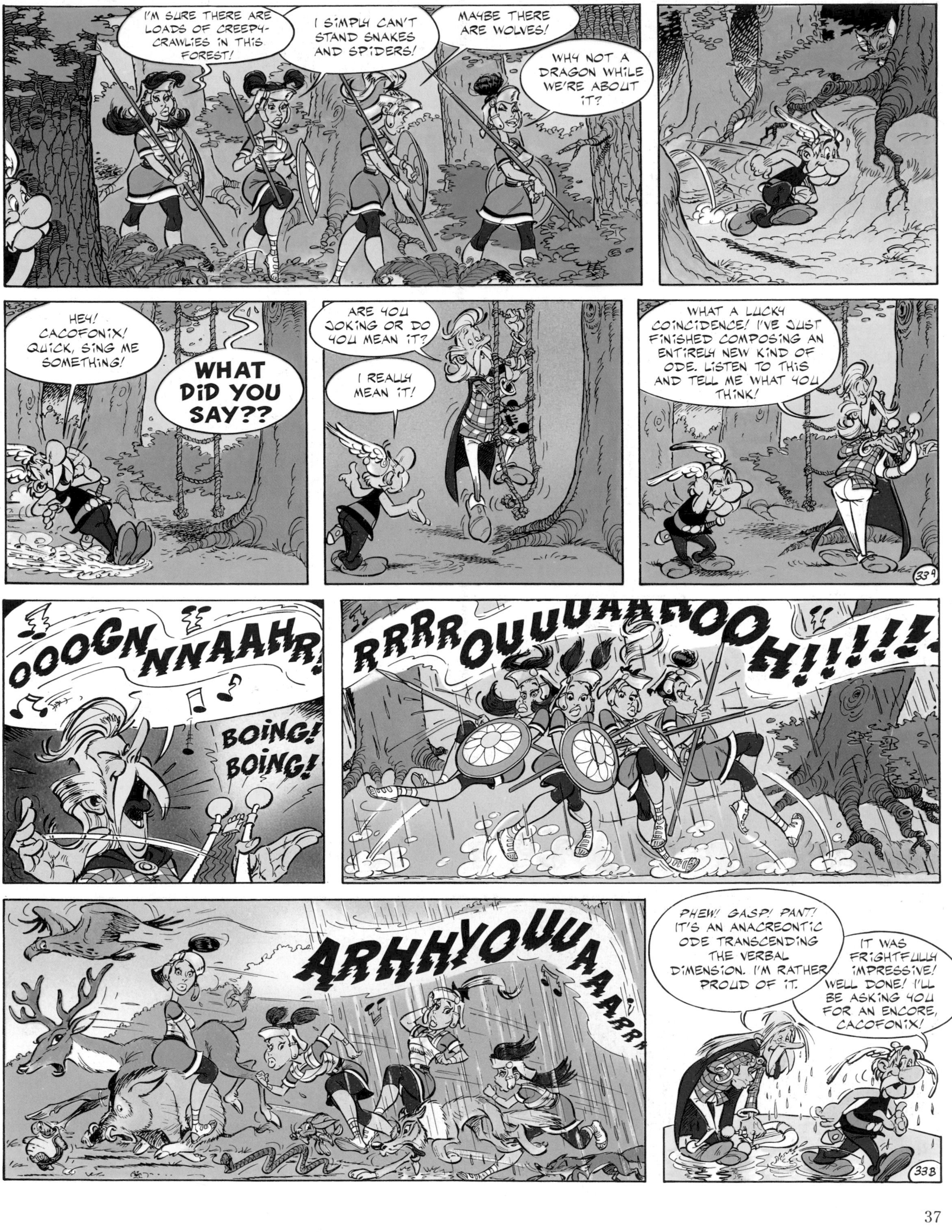
I'M SURE THERE ARE LOADS OF CREEPY-CRAWLIES IN THIS FOREST!
I SIMPLY CAN'T STAND SNAKES AND SPIDERS!
MAYBE THERE ARE WOLVES!
WHY NOT A DRAGON WHILE WE'RE ABOUT IT?
HEY! CACOFONIX! QUICK, SING ME SOMETHING!
WHAT DID YOU SAY??
ARE YOU JOKING OR DO YOU MEAN IT?
I REALLY MEAN IT!
WHAT A LUCKY COINCIDENCE! I'VE JUST FINISHED COMPOSING AN ENTIRELY NEW KIND OF ODE. LISTEN TO THIS AND TELL ME WHAT YOU THINK!
33 9
OOOGN NNAAHR!
BOING! BOING!
RRRROUUUAAHOOH!!!!!!
ARHHYOUUAAARR!
PHEW! GASP! PANT! IT'S AN ANACREONTIC ODE TRANSCENDING THE VERBAL DIMENSION. I'M RATHER PROUD OF IT.
IT WAS FRIGHTFULLY IMPRESSIVE! WELL DONE! I'LL BE ASKING YOU FOR AN ENCORE, CACOFONIX!
33 B

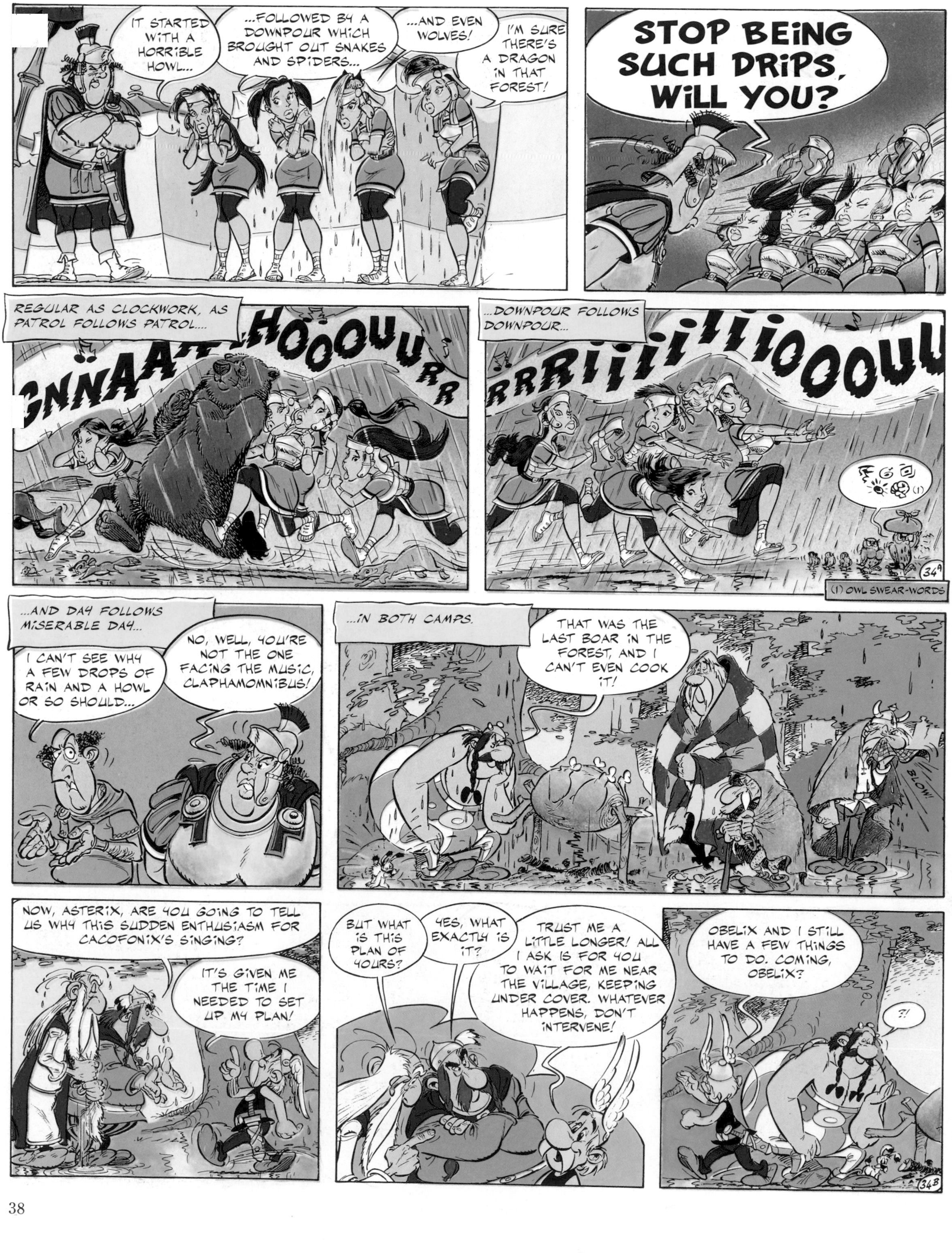

IT STARTED WITH A HORRIBLE HOWL...
...FOLLOWED BY A DOWNPOUR WHICH BROUGHT OUT SNAKES AND SPIDERS...
...AND EVEN WOLVES!
I'M SURE THERE'S A DRAGON IN THAT FOREST!
STOP BEING SUCH DRIPS, WILL YOU?
REGULAR AS CLOCKWORK, AS PATROL FOLLOWS PATROL....
GNNAAAHHOOOOUUURR
...DOWNPOUR FOLLOWS DOWNPOUR...
RRRIIIIIIIOOOOUU
(1) OWL SWEAR-WORDS
...AND DAY FOLLOWS MISERABLE DAY...
I CAN'T SEE WHY A FEW DROPS OF RAIN AND A HOWL OR SO SHOULD...
NO, WELL, YOU'RE NOT THE ONE FACING THE MUSIC, CLAPHAMOMNIBUS!
...IN BOTH CAMPS.
THAT WAS THE LAST BOAR IN THE FOREST, AND I CAN'T EVEN COOK IT!
BLOW!
NOW, ASTERIX, ARE YOU GOING TO TELL US WHY THIS SUDDEN ENTHUSIASM FOR CACOFONIX'S SINGING?
IT'S GIVEN ME THE TIME I NEEDED TO SET UP MY PLAN!
BUT WHAT IS THIS PLAN OF YOURS?
YES, WHAT EXACTLY IS IT?
TRUST ME A LITTLE LONGER! ALL I ASK IS FOR YOU TO WAIT FOR ME NEAR THE VILLAGE, KEEPING UNDER COVER. WHATEVER HAPPENS, DON'T INTERVENE!
OBELIX AND I STILL HAVE A FEW THINGS TO DO. COMING, OBELIX?
?!

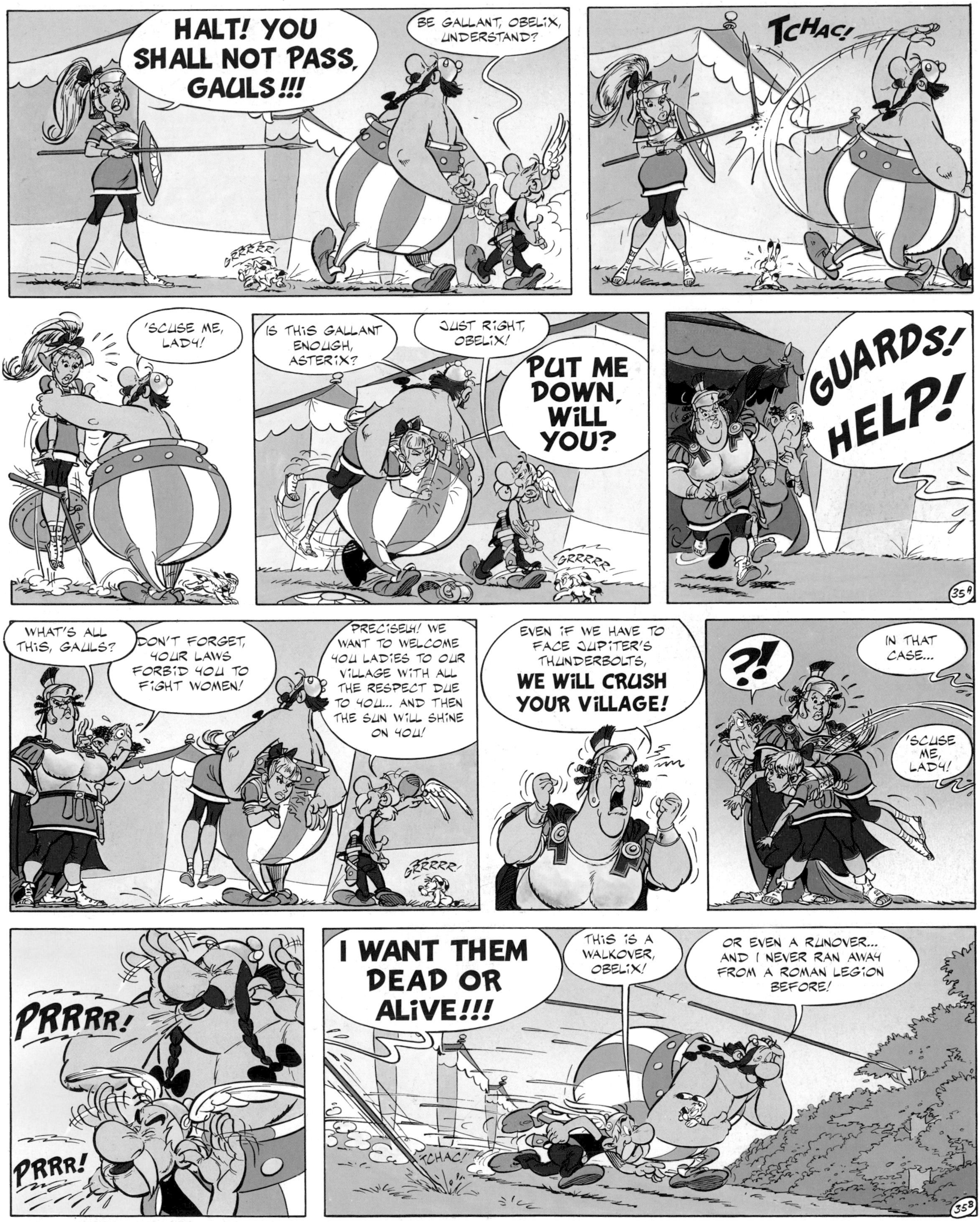
HALT! YOU SHALL NOT PASS, GAULS!!!
BE GALLANT, OBELIX, UNDERSTAND?
GRRRRR!
TCHAC!
'SCUSE ME, LADY!
IS THIS GALLANT ENOUGH, ASTERIX?
JUST RIGHT, OBELIX!
PUT ME DOWN, WILL YOU?
GRRRRR!
GUARDS! HELP!
35A
WHAT'S ALL THIS, GAULS?
DON'T FORGET, YOUR LAWS FORBID YOU TO FIGHT WOMEN!
PRECISELY! WE WANT TO WELCOME YOU LADIES TO OUR VILLAGE WITH ALL THE RESPECT DUE TO YOU... AND THEN THE SUN WILL SHINE ON YOU!
GRRRRR!
EVEN IF WE HAVE TO FACE JUPITER'S THUNDERBOLTS, WE WILL CRUSH YOUR VILLAGE!
?!
IN THAT CASE...
'SCUSE ME, LADY!
PRRRR!
PRRR!
I WANT THEM DEAD OR ALIVE!!!
THIS IS A WALKOVER, OBELIX!
OR EVEN A RUNOVER... AND I NEVER RAN AWAY FROM A ROMAN LEGION BEFORE!
TCHAC!
35B

WHAT A SHAME! I COULD HAVE BROUGHT THE FOREST DOWN!
...AND CAESAR WILL ASK ME: 'QUID NOVI, FILI?'(1) AND I'LL SAY: 'VENI, VIDI, VICI!'(2) AND THEN HE'LL MAKE ME A SENATOR!
(1) WHAT NEWS, SON?
(2) I CAME, I SAW, I CONQUERED!
SHOW THESE GAULISH BARBARIANS THE TRUE STRENGTH OF THE ROMAN LEGIONS: THEIR ABILITY TO FIGHT WITH ORDER AND DISCIPLINE!
CHAAARGE!
WEEEEEEEEEEEEEEEEEEEEEEEEEEE
BY JUPITER, THAT'LL SHOW 'EM!
WEEEEEEE
WHY THIS SUDDEN SILENCE? I HOPE THE GAULS HAVE BEEN GALLANT!
???????

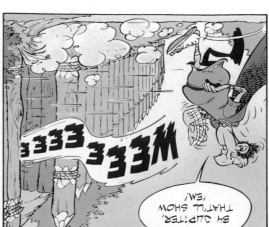

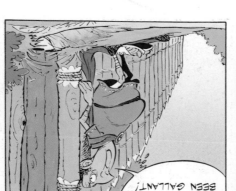

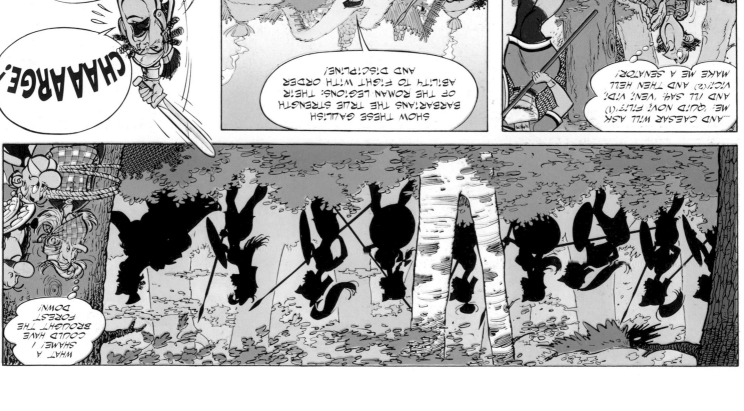

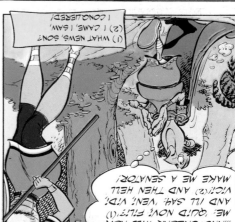

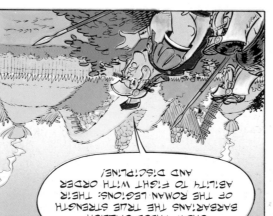

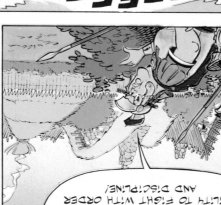

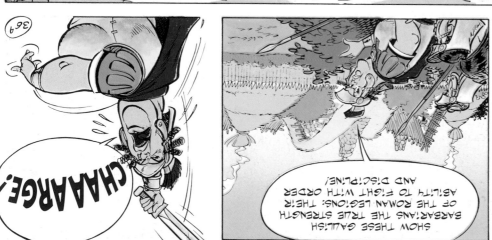

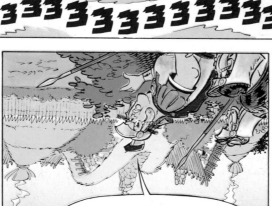

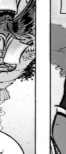

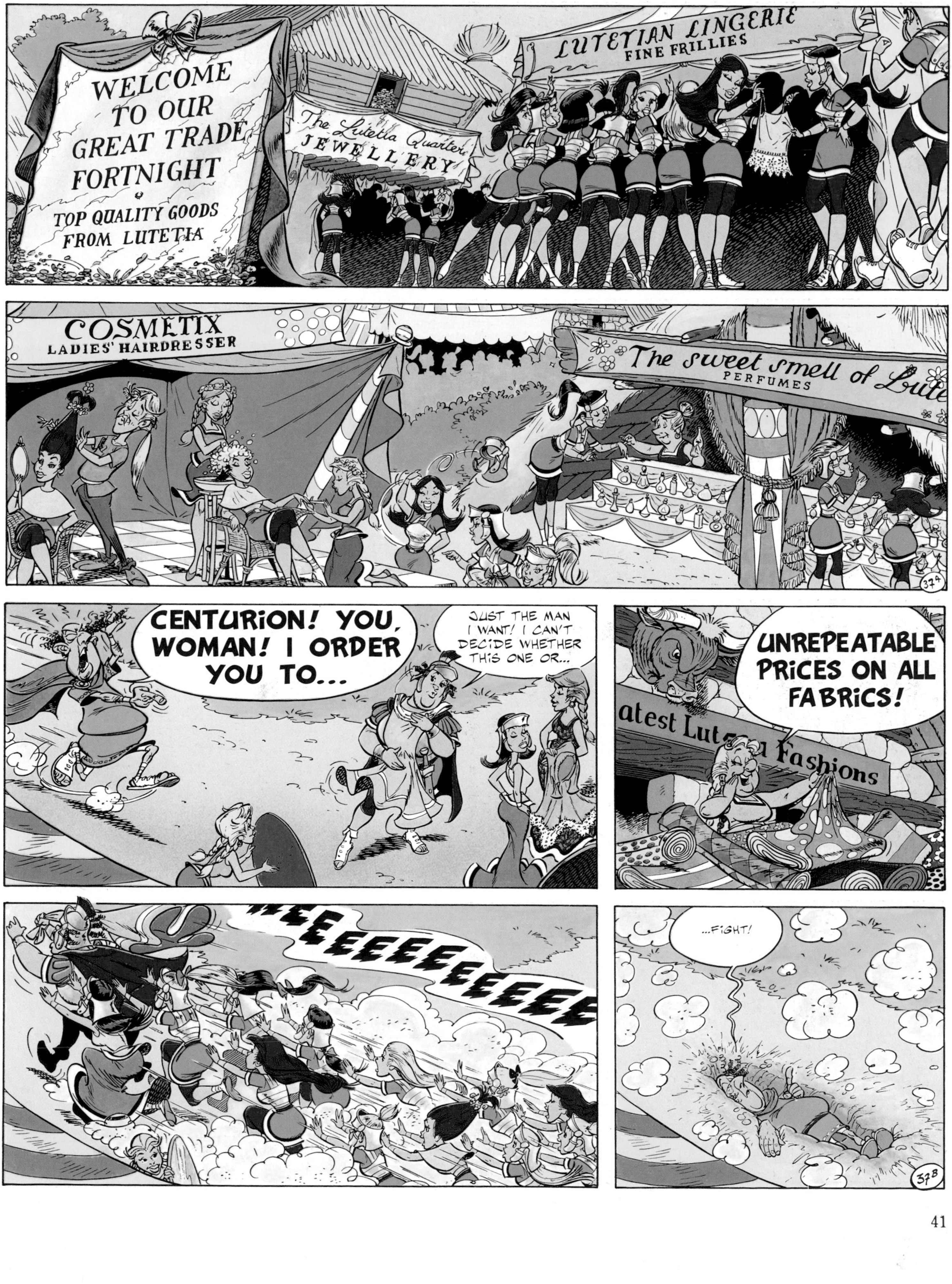
WELCOME TO OUR GREAT TRADE FORTNIGHT
TOP QUALITY GOODS FROM LUTETIA
The Lutetia Quarter JEWELLERY
LUTETIAN LINGERIE
FINE FRILLIES
COSMETIX
LADIES' HAIRDRESSER
PERFUMES
CENTURION! YOU, WOMAN! I ORDER YOU TO...
JUST THE MAN I WANT! I CAN'T DECIDE WHETHER THIS ONE OR...
UNREPEATABLE PRICES ON ALL FABRICS!
...FIGHT!

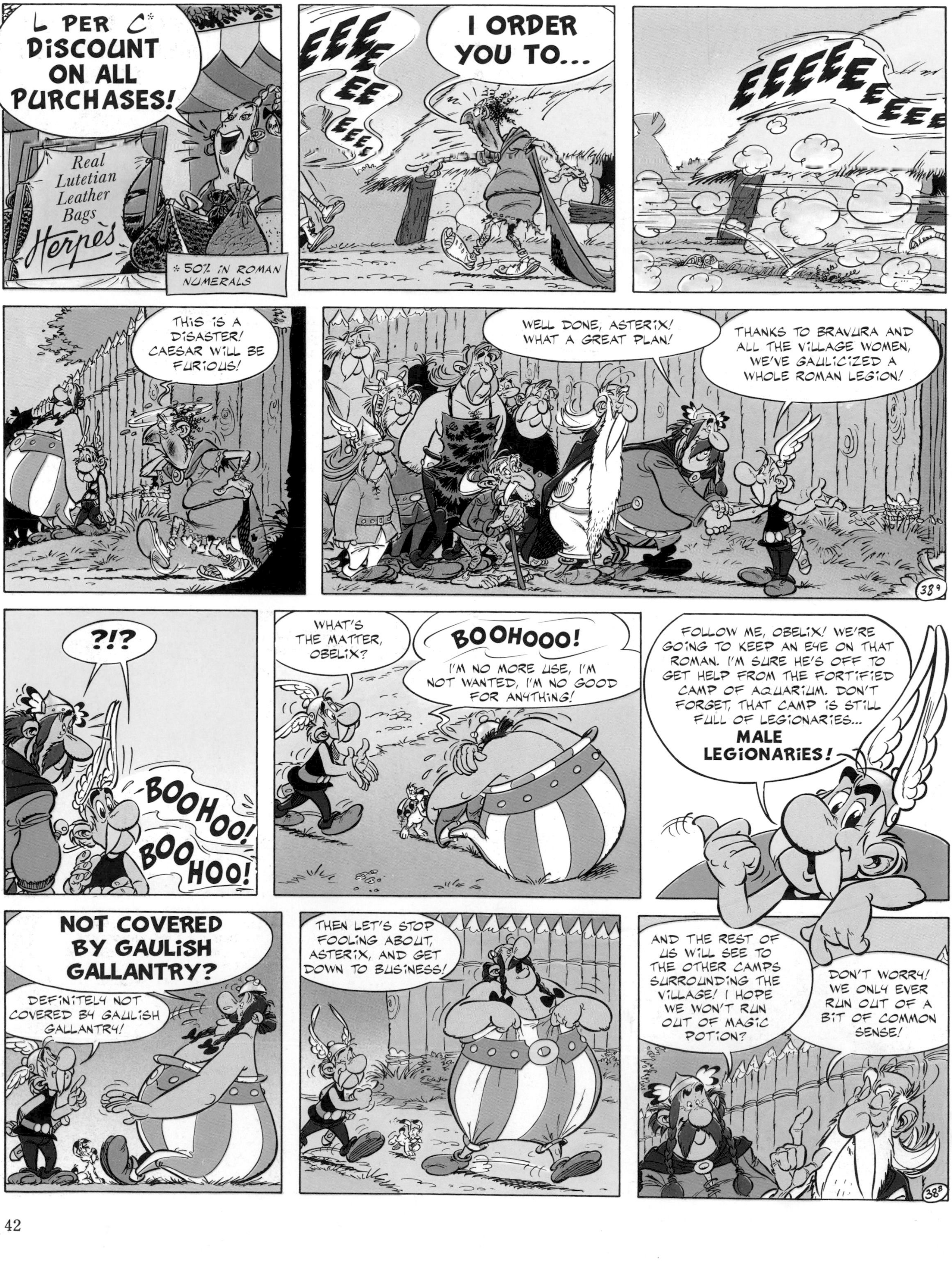
L PER C* DISCOUNT ON ALL PURCHASES!
Real Lutetian Leather Bags
Herpès
*50% IN ROMAN NUMERALS
EEEEEEEEEE
I ORDER YOU TO...
EEEEEEEEEE
THIS IS A DISASTER! CAESAR WILL BE FURIOUS!
WELL DONE, ASTERIX! WHAT A GREAT PLAN!
THANKS TO BRAVURA AND ALL THE VILLAGE WOMEN, WE'VE GAULICIZED A WHOLE ROMAN LEGION!
?!?
BOOHOO! BOOHOO!
WHAT'S THE MATTER, OBELIX?
BOOHOOO!
I'M NO MORE USE, I'M NOT WANTED, I'M NO GOOD FOR ANYTHING!
FOLLOW ME, OBELIX! WE'RE GOING TO KEEP AN EYE ON THAT ROMAN. I'M SURE HE'S OFF TO GET HELP FROM THE FORTIFIED CAMP OF AQUARIUM. DON'T FORGET, THAT CAMP IS STILL FULL OF LEGIONARIES... MALE LEGIONARIES!
NOT COVERED BY GAULISH GALLANTRY?
DEFINITELY NOT COVERED BY GAULISH GALLANTRY!
THEN LET'S STOP FOOLING ABOUT, ASTERIX, AND GET DOWN TO BUSINESS!
AND THE REST OF US WILL SEE TO THE OTHER CAMPS SURROUNDING THE VILLAGE! I HOPE WE WON'T RUN OUT OF MAGIC POTION?
DON'T WORRY! WE ONLY EVER RUN OUT OF A BIT OF COMMON SENSE!

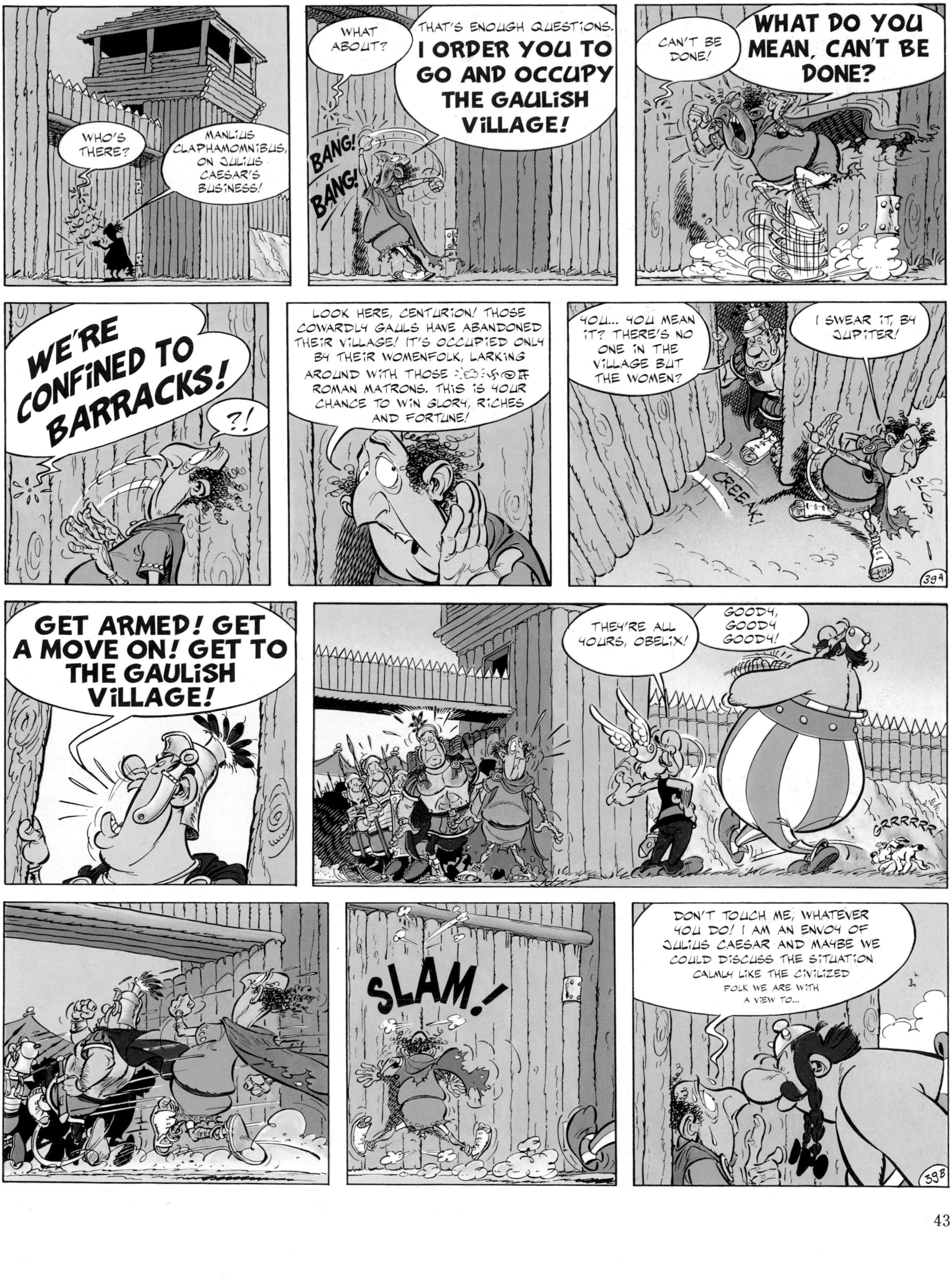

WHO'S THERE?
MANLIUS CLAPHAMOMNIBUS, ON JULIUS CAESAR'S BUSINESS!
KNOCK! KNOCK! KNOCK!
WHAT ABOUT?
THAT'S ENOUGH QUESTIONS. I ORDER YOU TO GO AND OCCUPY THE GAULISH VILLAGE!
BANG! BANG!
CAN'T BE DONE!
WHAT DO YOU MEAN, CAN'T BE DONE?
WE'RE CONFINED TO BARRACKS!
?!
LOOK HERE, CENTURION! THOSE COWARDLY GAULS HAVE ABANDONED THEIR VILLAGE! IT'S OCCUPIED ONLY BY THEIR WOMENFOLK, LARKING AROUND WITH THOSE ROMAN MATRONS. THIS IS YOUR CHANCE TO WIN GLORY, RICHES AND FORTUNE!
YOU... YOU MEAN IT? THERE'S NO ONE IN THE VILLAGE BUT THE WOMEN?
I SWEAR IT, BY JUPITER!
CREEAK!
SLUP!
GET ARMED! GET A MOVE ON! GET TO THE GAULISH VILLAGE!
THEY'RE ALL YOURS, OBELIX!
GOODY, GOODY GOODY!
GRRRRRR!
SLAM!
DON'T TOUCH ME, WHATEVER YOU DO! I AM AN ENVOY OF JULIUS CAESAR AND MAYBE WE COULD DISCUSS THE SITUATION CALMLY LIKE THE CIVILIZED FOLK WE ARE WITH A VIEW TO...

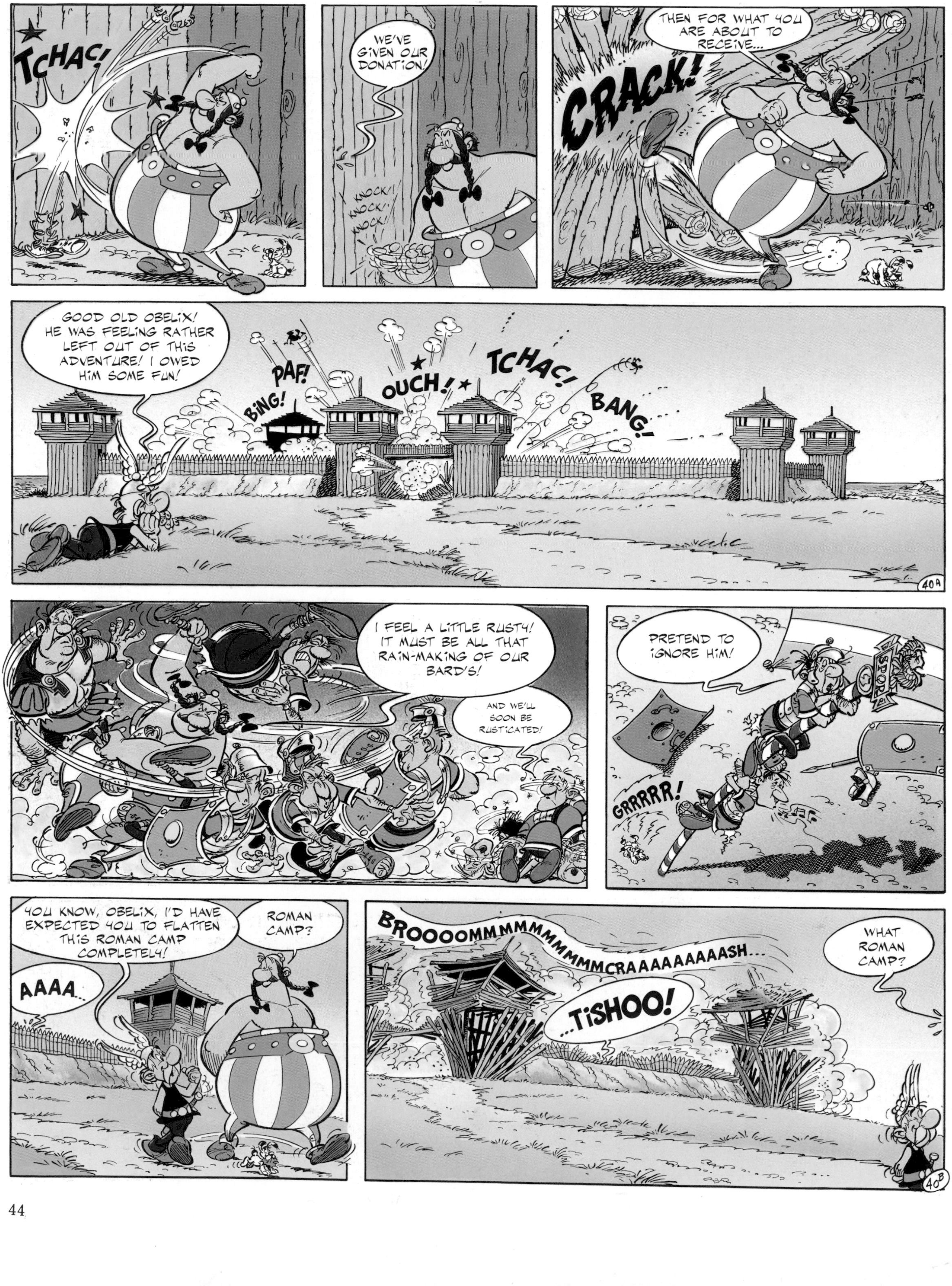
TCHAC!
WE'VE GIVEN OUR DONATION!
KNOCK! KNOCK! KNOCK!
THEN FOR WHAT YOU ARE ABOUT TO RECEIVE...
CRACK!
GOOD OLD OBELIX! HE WAS FEELING RATHER LEFT OUT OF THIS ADVENTURE! I OWED HIM SOME FUN!
BING!
PAF!
OUCH!
TCHAC!
BANG!
40A
I FEEL A LITTLE RUSTY! IT MUST BE ALL THAT RAIN-MAKING OF OUR BARD'S!
AND WE'LL SOON BE RUSTICATED!
PRETEND TO IGNORE HIM!
SPQR
GRRRRR!
YOU KNOW, OBELIX, I'D HAVE EXPECTED YOU TO FLATTEN THIS ROMAN CAMP COMPLETELY!
ROMAN CAMP?
AAAA...
BROOOOMMMMMMMMMMCRAAAAAAAAASH...
...TISHOO!
WHAT ROMAN CAMP?
40B

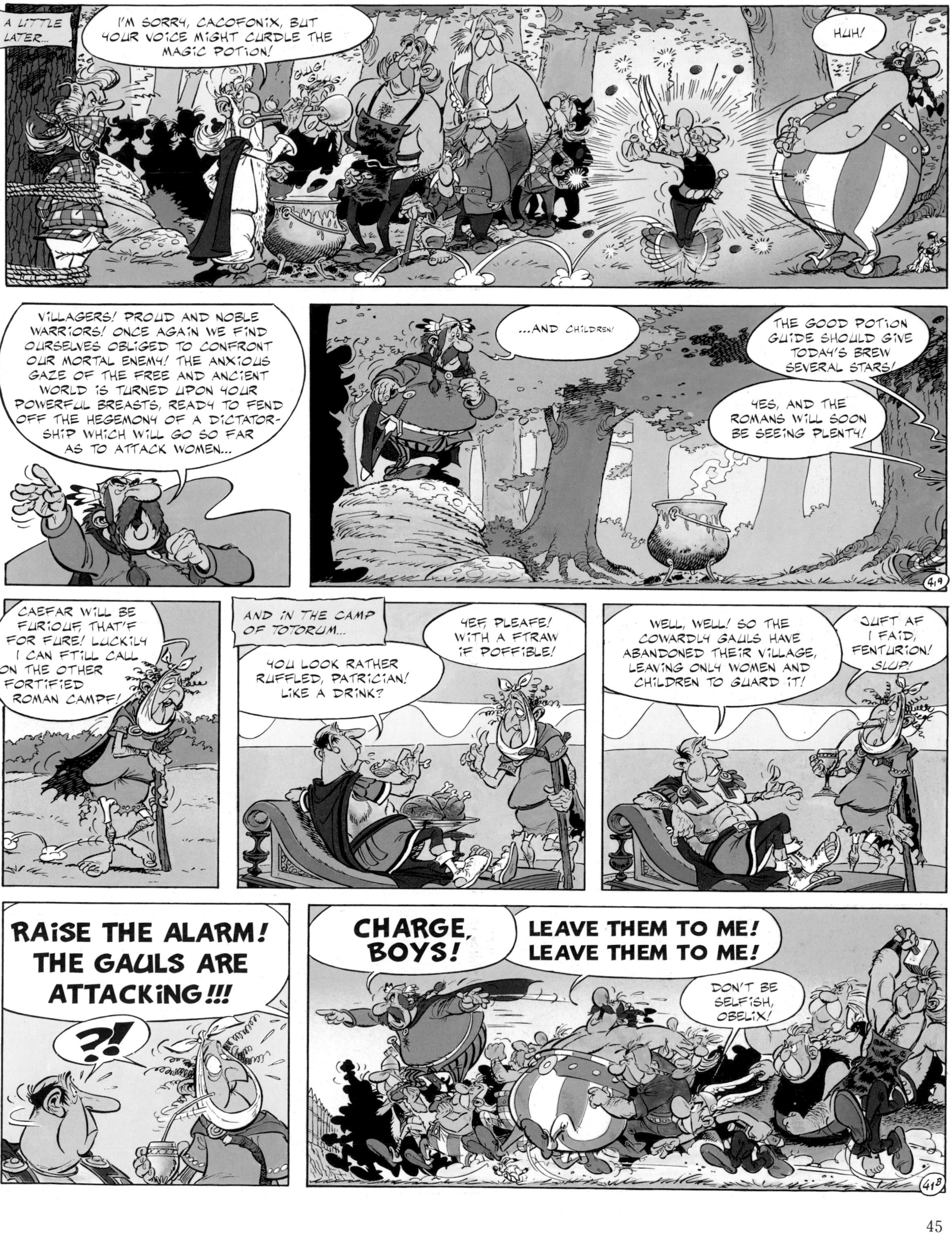
A LITTLE LATER...
I'M SORRY, CACOFONIX, BUT YOUR VOICE MIGHT CURDLE THE MAGIC POTION!
GLUG! GLUG!
HUH!
VILLAGERS! PROUD AND NOBLE WARRIORS! ONCE AGAIN WE FIND OURSELVES OBLIGED TO CONFRONT OUR MORTAL ENEMY! THE ANXIOUS GAZE OF THE FREE AND ANCIENT WORLD IS TURNED UPON YOUR POWERFUL BREASTS, READY TO FEND OFF THE HEGEMONY OF A DICTATORSHIP WHICH WILL GO SO FAR AS TO ATTACK WOMEN...
...AND CHILDREN!
THE GOOD POTION GUIDE SHOULD GIVE TODAY'S BREW SEVERAL STARS!
YES, AND THE ROMANS WILL SOON BE SEEING PLENTY!
CAEFAR WILL BE FURIOUF, THAT'F FOR FURE! LUCKILY I CAN FTILL CALL ON THE OTHER FORTIFIED ROMAN CAMPF!
AND IN THE CAMP OF TOTORUM...
YOU LOOK RATHER RUFFLED, PATRICIAN! LIKE A DRINK?
YEF, PLEAFE! WITH A FTRAW IF POFFIBLE!
WELL, WELL! SO THE COWARDLY GAULS HAVE ABANDONED THEIR VILLAGE, LEAVING ONLY WOMEN AND CHILDREN TO GUARD IT!
JUFT AF I FAID, FENTURION! SLUP!
RAISE THE ALARM! THE GAULS ARE ATTACKING!!!
?!
CHARGE, BOYS!
LEAVE THEM TO ME! LEAVE THEM TO ME!
DON'T BE SELFISH, OBELIX!

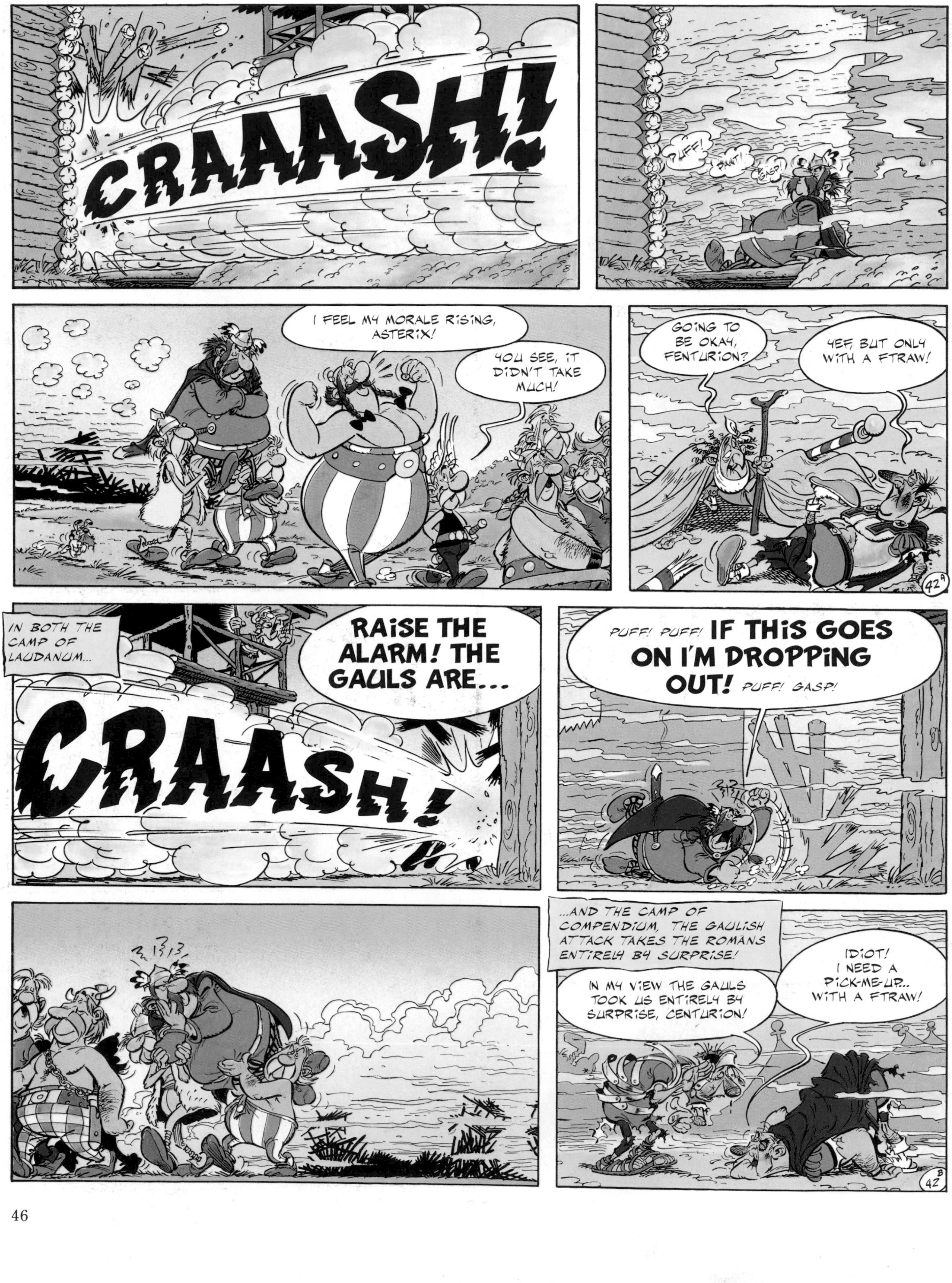
CRAAASH!
PUFF!
PANT!
GASP!
I FEEL MY MORALE RISING, ASTERIX!
YOU SEE, IT DIDN'T TAKE MUCH!
GOING TO BE OKAY, FENTURION?
YEF, BUT ONLY WITH A FTRAW!
IN BOTH THE CAMP OF LAUDANUM...
RAISE THE ALARM! THE GAULS ARE...
CRAASH!
PUFF! PUFF! IF THIS GOES ON I'M DROPPING OUT! PUFF! GASP!
...AND THE CAMP OF COMPENDIUM, THE GAULISH ATTACK TAKES THE ROMANS ENTIRELY BY SURPRISE!
IN MY VIEW THE GAULS TOOK US ENTIRELY BY SURPRISE, CENTURION!
IDIOT! I NEED A PICK-ME-UP... WITH A FTRAW!

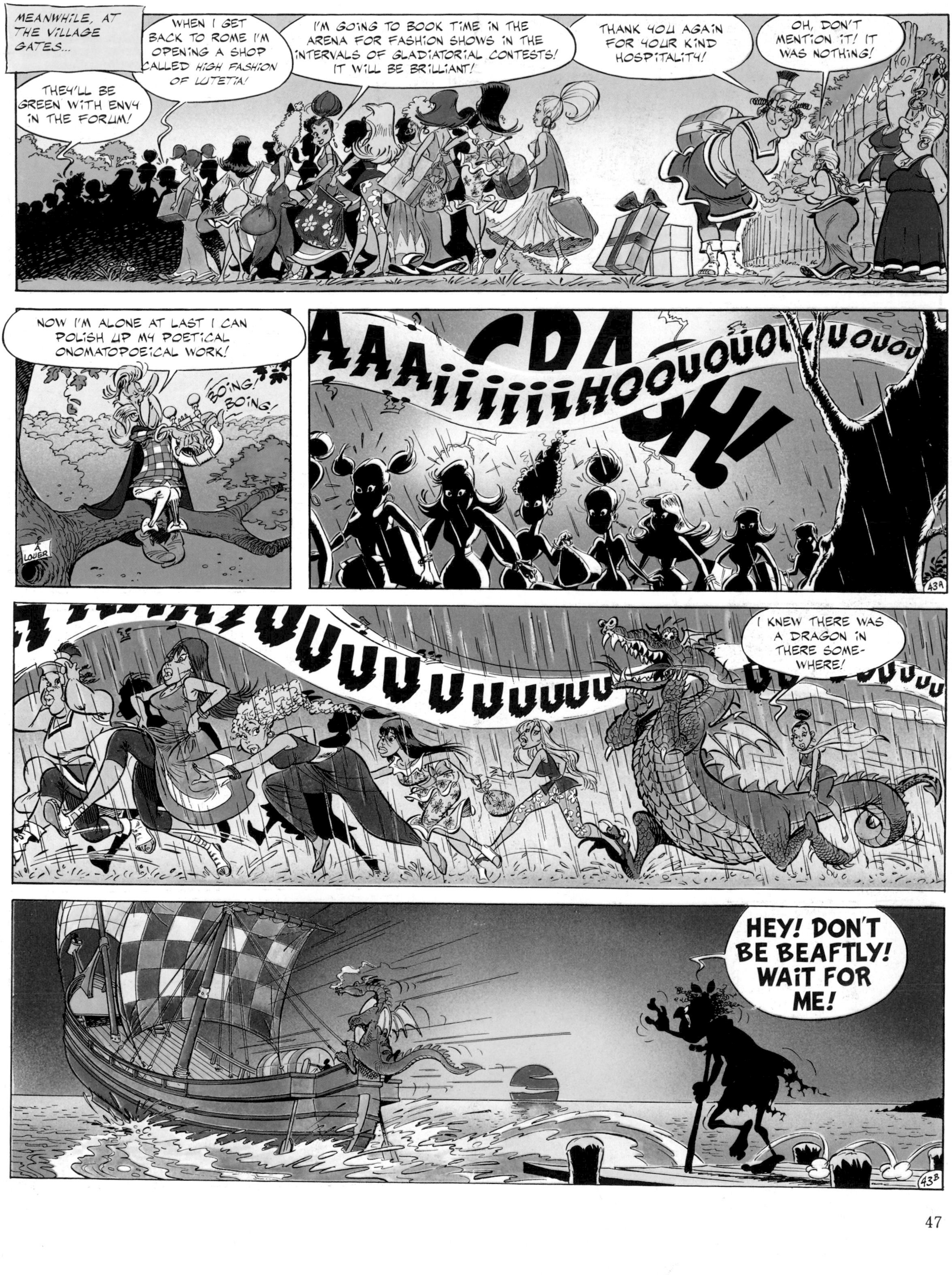
MEANWHILE, AT THE VILLAGE GATES...
THEY'LL BE GREEN WITH ENVY IN THE FORUM!
WHEN I GET BACK TO ROME I'M OPENING A SHOP CALLED HIGH FASHION OF LUTETIA!
I'M GOING TO BOOK TIME IN THE ARENA FOR FASHION SHOWS IN THE INTERVALS OF GLADIATORIAL CONTESTS! IT WILL BE BRILLIANT!
THANK YOU AGAIN FOR YOUR KIND HOSPITALITY!
OH, DON'T MENTION IT! IT WAS NOTHING!
NOW I'M ALONE AT LAST I CAN POLISH UP MY POETICAL ONOMATOPOEICAL WORK!
BOING! BOING!
À LOUER
I KNEW THERE WAS A DRAGON IN THERE SOMEWHERE!
HEY! DON'T BE BEAFTLY! WAIT FOR ME!

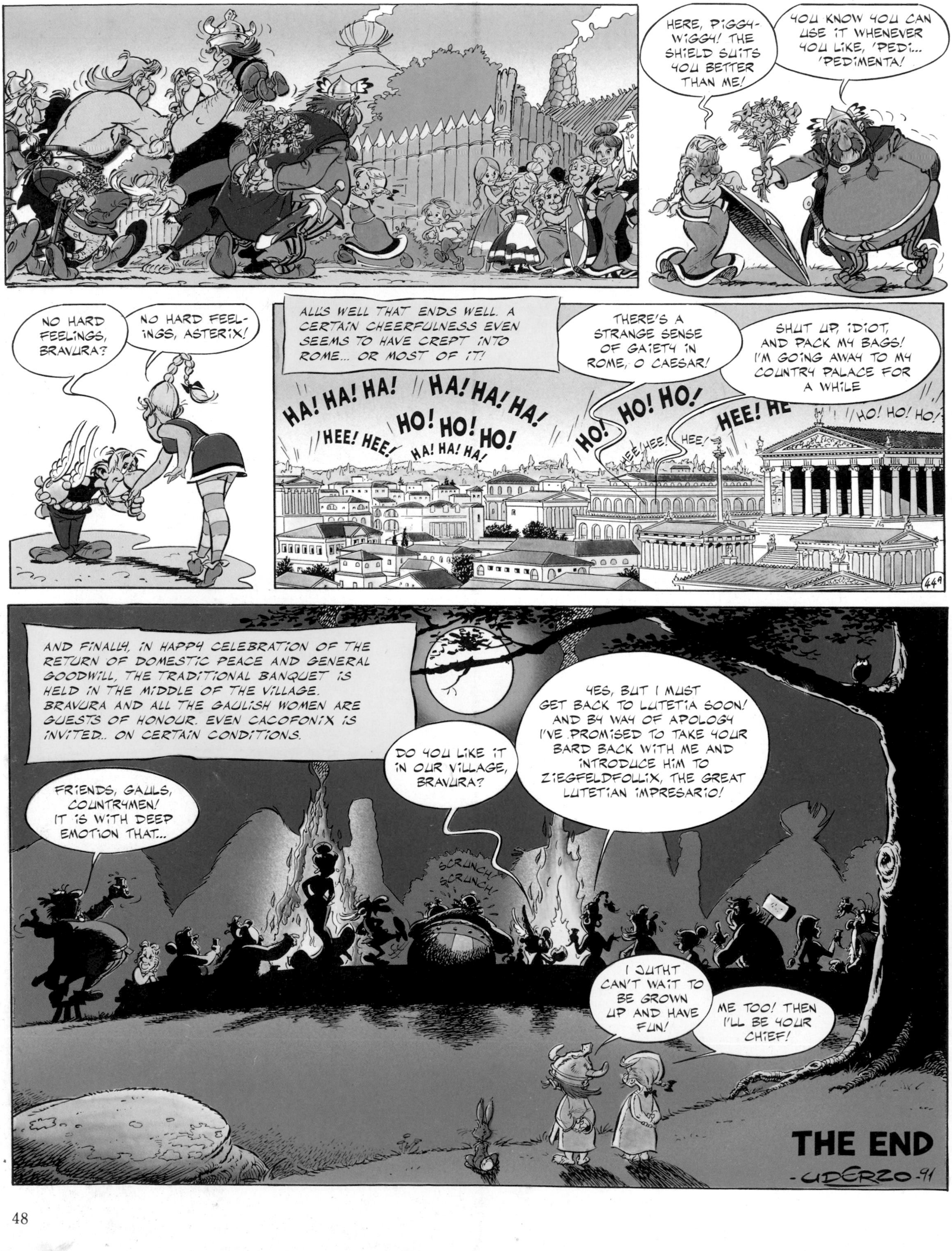
HERE, PIGGY-WIGGY! THE SHIELD SUITS YOU BETTER THAN ME!
YOU KNOW YOU CAN USE IT WHENEVER YOU LIKE, 'PEDI... 'PEDIMENTA!
NO HARD FEELINGS, BRAVURA?
NO HARD FEEL-INGS, ASTERIX!
ALL'S WELL THAT ENDS WELL. A CERTAIN CHEERFULNESS EVEN SEEMS TO HAVE CREPT INTO ROME... OR MOST OF IT!
THERE'S A STRANGE SENSE OF GAIETY IN ROME, O CAESAR!
SHUT UP, IDIOT, AND PACK MY BAGS! I'M GOING AWAY TO MY COUNTRY PALACE FOR A WHILE
HA! HA! HA! HA! HA! HA! HA! HEE! HEE! HO! HO! HO! HA! HA! HA! HO! HO! HO! HEE! HEE! HEE! HEE! HE HO! HO! HO!
AND FINALLY, IN HAPPY CELEBRATION OF THE RETURN OF DOMESTIC PEACE AND GENERAL GOODWILL, THE TRADITIONAL BANQUET IS HELD IN THE MIDDLE OF THE VILLAGE. BRAVURA AND ALL THE GAULISH WOMEN ARE GUESTS OF HONOUR. EVEN CACOFONIX IS INVITED.. ON CERTAIN CONDITIONS.
FRIENDS, GAULS, COUNTRYMEN! IT IS WITH DEEP EMOTION THAT...
DO YOU LIKE IT IN OUR VILLAGE, BRAVURA?
YES, BUT I MUST GET BACK TO LUTETIA SOON! AND BY WAY OF APOLOGY I'VE PROMISED TO TAKE YOUR BARD BACK WITH ME AND INTRODUCE HIM TO ZIEGFELDFOLLIX, THE GREAT LUTETIAN IMPRESARIO!
SCRUNCH SCRUNCH
I JUTHT CAN'T WAIT TO BE GROWN UP AND HAVE FUN!
ME TOO! THEN I'LL BE YOUR CHIEF!
THE END
-UDERZO-91